The mist r
obscured ~~the view of land,~~
kind of how Sam felt about this case.

And if he didn't get his bearings soon, he might just run aground. The fact that almost getting killed hadn't been enough to convince Jen to divulge her secrets made it look as though she was neck-deep in the art fraud.

On the other side of the balcony divider, he heard Jen cry out. He scaled the balcony rail, swung around the partition and hurried to her side as she wrestled a blanket in her lounge chair.

"Jen," he whispered. "It's just a dream. You're okay. Wake up."

Her eyes flew open. "Sam? What are you doing here?"

"You cried out. I thought you were in trouble."

"I must've been dreaming. Every time I close my eyes I see his face, see him lunging toward me." She shivered.

Against his better judgment, Sam folded her in his arms. He couldn't help himself. She looked utterly stricken. He wanted to say *It's okay. You're safe now.* But he didn't know that. In fact, he doubted it with every ounce of his being.

Books by Sandra Orchard

Love Inspired Suspense

*Deep Cover
*Shades of Truth
*Critical Condition
  Fatal Inheritance
  Perilous Waters

*Undercover Cops

SANDRA ORCHARD

hails from the beautiful countryside of Niagara, Ontario, where inspiration abounds for her romantic-suspense novels—not that she runs into any bad guys, but because her imagination is free to run as wild as her Iditarod-wannabe husky. Sandra lives with her real-life hero husband, who happily provides both romantic and suspense inspiration, as long as it doesn't involve poisons and his dinner. But her truest inspiration comes from the Lord, in the beauty of a sunrise over the field and the whisper of a breeze, in the antics of a killdeer determined to safeguard its nest and the faithfulness of the seasons. She enjoys writing stories that both keep the reader guessing and reveal God's love and faithfulness through the lives of her characters.

Sandra loves to hear from readers and can be reached through her website, or at www.Facebook.com/SandraOrchard or c/o Love Inspired Books, 233 Broadway, Suite 1001, New York, NY 10279.

PERILOUS WATERS

SANDRA ORCHARD

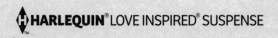
HARLEQUIN® LOVE INSPIRED® SUSPENSE

Recycling programs
for this product may
not exist in your area.

™ LOVE INSPIRED BOOKS

ISBN-13: 978-0-373-67603-3

PERILOUS WATERS

Copyright © 2014 by Sandra van den Bogerd

www.Harlequin.com

Printed in U.S.A.

When you pass through the waters,
I will be with you; and when you pass through
the rivers, they will not sweep over you.
—*Isaiah* 43:2

To my husband, my favorite person with whom
to celebrate life's special moments.

Acknowledgments

Thank you to my daughter Christine for patiently
deciphering and typing my handwritten manuscript.
Words flow much faster from a pen than a keyboard
for me. Thank you to my faithful accountability
partner and prayer warrior, Patti Jo Moore,
for helping me through the rough spots.
And thank you to my critiquers—Wenda Dottridge,
Vicki McCollum, and Stacey Weeks—whose
unique insights enriched the story in many ways.

ONE

"Please tell me those women aren't why you're really in town."

Sam Steele shifted his gaze from the gorgeous heiresses dining in the corner of the dimly lit Seattle bistro and grinned at his brother. "They're not why I'm in town."

Jake's eyes narrowed. "*Right*. Now tell me the truth."

"What?" Sam brandished his most offended tone, hoping not to give away that Jake had nailed his mission. "Can't I look at a pretty woman?" *Pretty* hardly did Jennifer Robbins justice. His fingers itched to tug her blond locks free of the tidy bun she'd tamed them into.

"Sure, but I thought you gave up women after that jezebel almost cost you your job."

Sam gritted his teeth at the reminder of the woman he'd blithely dated for weeks until she'd manipulated him into being late for a rendezvous with a critical informant, who'd later turned up dead, and he'd had to prove he was merely a gullible idiot and not complicit in the plot.

Sam forced his shoulders to relax, sipped his water.

"Still a sore spot, I see." Jake smirked. "Want me to ask the twins to join us?"

"You know them?" The question came out strangled. Investigating women his brother knew would *not* go over well with his family, or his boss.

"The heiresses to the Robbins Art Gallery?" Jake said in a do-I-look-like-I-was-born-yesterday tone. "Everyone in Seattle knows them."

Sam leaned forward, holding his brother's x-ray-vision gaze without so much as a flinch. "They're not why I'm in town. I'm here to join our parents, you and my adorable nephew Tommy on an Alaskan cruise. Remember?"

Jake studied him a moment longer but thankfully didn't question Sam's sudden generosity in surprising them with the cruise tickets. He probably didn't want to risk being asked to pitch in. Jake drew back his hands, palms out. "Okay, I believe you."

No, he didn't. Bringing Jake here tonight had been a mistake. He knew Sam specialized in the FBI's art crime investigations, so he was bound to be more suspicious than ever when they "ran into" the women on the cruise next week.

Jake glanced over his shoulder again.

This time the twin sister, Cassandra, noticed and offered an inviting smile.

Terrific. Just what Sam didn't want. Now *she'd* be

suspicious of them on the cruise, too. Could anything else go wrong?

"Wipe that smirk off your face," Sam ordered. "Mom would kill you if you brought home a girl like that."

The corner of Jake's mouth hitched higher. "So I guess that means you'd prefer the more conservative-looking one? Her name's Jennifer, in case you're interested."

Yeah, but Sam didn't let on that he already knew. He knew more about the pair than Jake could imagine. Like the fact that their parents died in a tragic car accident when the girls were seventeen. That their former guardian, longtime family friend and gallery curator, Reginald Michaels, was their estate trustee until their twenty-fifth birthdays. That, although identical twins, the two women couldn't be more different.

Cassandra wore too much makeup, and flashy designer outfits that revealed more than they concealed. Meanwhile, Jennifer was as buttoned-up as they came in her navy suit and sensible shoes. She didn't seem to favor the nightclub photo ops like her sister, either. In fact, in the few publicity shots Sam had managed to dig up of the reclusive twin, her gaze held a lost-soul quality that had tugged at something deep inside him.

He shook away the thought. He shouldn't be noticing a suspect's ocean-blue eyes, except to be able to identify her in a lineup.

"She goes to church," his brother said, with a hint of amusement. "Has been going for a while."

"Good to know," Sam acknowledged, letting Jake have his fun if it meant diverting him from Sam's true interest in the women. But the backhanded reference to Ms. Jezebel stung. She'd orchestrated their acquaintance at his church, and because she hadn't seemed to have any affiliation to any of his cases, he'd trusted her far too easily. A mistake he never planned to repeat. "And you know this how?" Sam asked, suddenly curious how Jake happened to know so much about the women who were supposed to be out of their league.

Jake leaned back and took a long draw of his ginger ale before answering. "She goes to the same church as the fire chief."

Sam steeled himself against a spark of doubt about the woman's guilt. Jennifer might not work at the gallery like her sister, but as part owner, she'd have some inkling of their illegal dealings. Why else would her computer's IP address and cell phone have logged as many as six searches of the FBI's National Stolen Art Information Registry in the past week and a half—the last one while she was in the gallery earlier this evening?

According to the Anchorage office, the tip that a stolen Native American painting had surfaced in a Skagway gallery came from a reliable source. A wiretap on the gallery's phone had logged several suspicious calls from the Robbins Gallery. Two days later, Cassandra and Jennifer were booked on an Alaskan cruise.

Across the bistro, the women asked for their bill.

Sam pushed aside his half-finished dessert. "You done?"

Jake shoveled tiramisu into his mouth and shook his head.

The women stood, and Jake must've guessed at Sam's real reason for asking. Well, hopefully not the *real,* real reason.

Reginald Michaels's suspiciously worded conversations with the Skagway gallery had convinced Sam the twins' roles would be pivotal in smuggling the pieces south. He needed to know for sure.

In his six years on the FBI's art crime team, Sam had specialized in recovering stolen art, usually by posing as an unscrupulous private collector willing to overlook a masterpiece's provenance for the opportunity to own it. First he'd cultivate the seller's trust, then he'd set up the buy, and a combined team of FBI agents and local law enforcement would have his back. But time hadn't been on his side in this case.

Jake shoveled in another mouthful then quickly wiped his face. "Okay. I'm good."

By the time Sam paid the bill, the women had just about made it to their car, which was perfect because Sam could say bye to Jake and quietly tail the pair to their next destination. The late-June sun was sinking fast, which would make it easier to follow unobserved.

A scream split the air. One of the twins.

Jake hoofed across the parking lot with Sam on his heels, more than a little uneasy about meeting the twins this way. When he was close enough to see they were unharmed, he slowed and let his brother take the lead. The last thing he needed on this case was more complications.

"Are you two okay?" Jake asked.

The women, clearly shaken, both nodded.

Keeping his distance, Sam rounded behind them, taking in the slashed tires and the smashed driver-side window of the Ford Focus. An economy car. Another of the heiresses' anomalies.

Jake pulled out his cell phone. "Did you see who did this?"

"No, but—" Jennifer's voice wobbled as she reached through her shattered car window "—he left this."

"Don't touch it!" Moving in quickly to intervene, Sam caught her arm. The sheer panic in her eyes sliced off his breath. That and the ivory-handled knife pinning a torn note to the driver's seat headrest. On the paper, blood-red letters said YOU'LL PAY.

A chill skittered down his neck. Oh, this was a big complication.

"Let go of me." Jennifer tried to jerk free of the man who'd appeared out of nowhere in the secluded parking lot. But he held her arm fast while Cassandra just stood and stared.

"Hold still. You're bleeding." The man pressed a tissue against her palm.

"What?" Jen glanced down at his hand holding hers so determinedly. *Oh.* He meant to help her. Heat rushed to her cheeks as she stopped resisting.

"I'm sorry I scared you," he said in a rumbly voice that soothed her frayed nerves. "The police might be able to get fingerprints off the knife and note."

"Of course, I wasn't thinking." All she'd been thinking about was the *A Duel After the Masked Ball* painting she'd spotted squirreled away in the gallery's back room tonight.

She tamped down her panic at the sight of the knife and the thought that it must be connected to the painting. A painting of a stabbing.

She shuddered at the memory of the image. She hadn't wanted to believe Uncle Reginald could be mixed up in anything illegal. She'd actually convinced herself that the person who'd told her as much—the man she hoped to soon sell her share of the gallery to—was just trying to scare her out of soliciting other offers. But then she'd spotted the *Duel* painting where it shouldn't have been.

It wasn't wildly valuable by art standards, but it *was* listed as stolen on the FBI's online database.

And for all she knew this threat could be some kind of revenge.

Her rescuer squeezed her hand, mercifully disrupting her spiraling suspicions. He had a bump on his nose like maybe it had once been broken. His sandy-brown hair curled over his ears, grazing his collar, and his three-day beard growth made him look like a rugged cowboy, except for the sports jacket. He searched her face. "Or do you already know who did this?"

At the apprehension shadowing his coffee-brown eyes, butterflies fluttered through her stomach. "I—"

"It's got to be one of those nutcase grant applicants!" her sister shrieked. "She assesses them for a charitable foundation. They're always threatening her when she turns down their applications." Cassandra waved her arms at Jennifer. "Tell them."

"Calm down." Jen fought to keep her tone low and even. "These gentlemen don't need to know that."

"Do you see the size of that knife?" Cassandra wailed, louder than before, thrusting her finger at it. "The guy's a whack job!" Her gaze darted to the bushes that edged the parking lot, and she finally lowered her voice. "For all we know, if these guys hadn't shown up, the creep might've jumped us, too."

Jennifer shivered. Maybe her sister was right. Maybe this didn't have anything to do with Reginald or the painting. When she broke the news to Lester this morning that his proposal hadn't met the foundation's grant qualifications, he'd been irate.

But he had to know that this was no way to change her mind. Threats like this would only land him in jail.

Her rescuer's grip tightened, drawing her from her thoughts, and she realized he was trying to still her trembling.

"If someone has threatened you, you need to tell the police when they arrive," he said, although he looked as though he wanted to press for those details himself.

Her gaze skittered from the endearing concern in

his eyes to the small frown curving his lips. She swallowed, not sure what had her feeling more off kilter, the note in her car or the man comforting her. She slipped her hand free of his hold. "Yes, thank you. I'll do that."

Turning away, she winced at the curious gazes of people spilling out of the restaurant. She hated being the center of attention at the best of times. If the press caught wind of this, they'd be haunting her for weeks.

The man must've noticed her distress because he immediately motioned them to move on. "Everything's okay, folks. Nothing to see here." The other man positioned himself in front of her car door, effectively blocking the view of the knife.

A few people craned their necks for a better look but then wandered off like the others.

"Thank you, Mr...." Jennifer whispered. "I'm sorry. I don't even know your name."

"Sam. Sam Tate." He motioned to the tall, lanky fellow guarding the car door. "And this is my brother, Jake. He's with the Stalwart Fire Department north of the city."

Jake dipped his head toward her. "Ma'am."

She could see the family resemblance in their faces, especially the kindness in their eyes, but other than that they seemed as different in appearance as she and her sister were in personality. "Pleased to meet you both. I'm Jennifer Robbins, and this is my sister, Cassandra."

"What's taking the police so long?" Cassie fretted. "It's going to be dark soon." She wrapped her arms around her middle and flitted her long lashes at the tall fireman. "You'll stay until they come. Won't you?"

Jake grinned. "Be happy to."

His brother didn't seem in a hurry to leave, either. He crouched down and studied the slashed tires as Jennifer silently thanked God for bringing these two Good Samaritans in their time of need.

Cassie paced. "What if this guy knows where you live, Jen? If only we were leaving on the cruise tomorrow. Then he wouldn't be able to find you."

"You're going on a cruise?" Jake asked. "Which one?"

"Alaskan. We're supposed to leave Monday." Jen frowned at the note's sinister threat. She hadn't agreed to go yet, but maybe getting out of town for a week would be a good thing.

"Alaska? No way." Awe filled Jake's voice. "Us, too. What are the chances?" He turned to Sam, eyebrow arched.

"The trip is a birthday gift from our uncle." Cassie flashed a photo-worthy grin. "We're twins."

"Cool. We're celebrating our folks' fortieth wedding anniversary." Jake hitched his thumb toward his brother. "Sam's treat."

A *wealthy* cowboy then? And generous. Not that Jen cared about a man's wealth. She just wasn't interested in any guy who only cared about hers. Which seemed to be every guy who gave her a second look. Maybe the rest were too intimidated by her bigger bank account. Too bad Ian hadn't been. He'd done his homework so well that she'd gullibly believed he wanted the private family life she craved. Right up until Uncle Reggie presented him with an ironclad prenuptial agreement to sign.

Cassie tugged on Jen's sleeve. "See, Jen, the cruise won't be just partiers. You have to come with me."

Sam turned to her, looking surprised. "You're thinking of turning down an Alaskan cruise?"

Jen shrugged. Maybe going away for a week would stop whoever did this from bothering her again. Except she couldn't shake the niggling feeling Uncle Reggie wanted her out of Seattle for a reason.

Like maybe he'd heard that she'd secretly found a buyer for the gallery come their twenty-fifth birthday...when he lost his veto power.

She'd wanted out from the day her parents died driving home from a gallery gala. And the desire had only intensified with every gold-digging suitor who'd knocked on her door since. Uncle Reggie had to know she'd act on it.

She sucked in a breath. *Two weeks.* And she still had to win Cassie's agreement to sell her half, too, for the deal to work. Which wouldn't be easy, considering Cass had worked at the gallery since high school and loved everything about it. The last thing Jen wanted to do was take that away from her. But finding that stolen painting tonight, and now this, changed everything.

She'd already lost her parents and scarcely saw Aunt Martha since she'd divorced Reg. Cass was the only family she had left. She couldn't bear to lose her, too. And she could, because if the deal fell through, it was only a matter of time before the police caught wind of what Reg was up to. And Cass would be implicated alongside him. Perhaps getting her away from him and the gallery for ten whole days might make it easier to win her over.

The wail of a police siren drew closer.

She sure wouldn't have another opportunity tonight to broach the subject.

Sam studied her, his head tilted, as if he couldn't figure out why anyone would turn down the gift of a cruise.

She chewed on her bottom lip.

If she went and won her sister's agreement, she'd still have two days to finalize the sale once they returned before the buyer's deadline expired. And she couldn't let it expire. Not now that she knew his warning wasn't just a scare tactic.

TWO

The fog didn't look like it'd lift any time soon…in more ways than one.

Sam stood at the ship's rail, scrutinizing the late-comers rushing up the gangplank as he listened to his deputy director on the other end of his cell phone. "It won't be a problem, sir," he assured.

"See that it's not."

Sam clenched his jaw. "Understood." He clicked off and shoved the phone into his pocket. The guy had been gunning for him ever since he showed him up on the Carlisle case.

And the fiasco with Jezebel—as his brother fondly called her—had given his boss the ammunition to take him out. He couldn't afford to mess up again, especially on a case with a couple of beautiful women involved.

Jake sidled up beside him and slapped him on the back. "Looking for a certain someone?"

"Just waiting for you guys," Sam said, refusing to rise to the bait.

"Right." Jake chuckled as his four-year-old son

bounced up and down, tugging on his arm, begging to explore the ship.

Sam pressed his fingertips to his forehead and massaged the dull throb that had been there since seeing that note in Jennifer's car.

"Hey, you okay?" Concern replaced the amusement in Jake's voice.

"Yeah." Sam dropped his hand and returned his attention to the wharf. He'd be a lot better if he knew who'd left Jennifer the note and why. Unlike her hysterical sister, Jennifer had kept a tight rein on her emotions, but he'd felt the tremble in her hand, seen the quiver in her lips. The guy had gotten to her. Thrown her off her game.

Maybe left her too spooked to make this trip.

"Hey, relax. You're supposed to be on vacation. Remember?"

Yeah. The other night when Jake questioned him about giving Jennifer his undercover name, Sam had told him it was a precaution. He posed as a buyer in the art world too often to be known to people in it by any other name. Jake clearly hadn't bought the excuse.

And Mom and Dad would not be impressed if he bailed on the trip.

But if Jennifer and Cassandra didn't board, he'd have no choice. He couldn't afford to let them off his radar.

Tommy tugged on Sam's pant leg. "Can we explore now?"

"Sure." Sam took one last look at the gangplank. "Where are Mom and Dad?"

"They headed up to the buffet for something to eat," Jake said. "I told them we'd meet them there."

"Hey, strangers!" a friendly female voice chimed from behind them.

"Look who's here." Jake leaned back, his arms resting on the rail, and nudged Sam's arm. "Good to see you."

Cassandra flounced toward them in a multicolored, artsy-looking getup with an uneven angular hem that reminded Sam of a court jester.

But when her sister didn't appear behind her, Sam didn't feel like laughing. "Jennifer's not coming?"

"Sure." The twinkly smile in Cassandra's eyes conveyed almost a giddy pleasure in his interest in her sister, which could nicely work to his favor. Cassandra fluttered her hand in the direction she'd come. "She just wanted to make a few phone calls before we left port and lost cell phone reception. I'm meeting her at the buffet in twenty minutes."

"That's where we're headed, too," Jake piped up. "Would you like to join us?"

"Love to." She hooked her arm through Jake's. "Do you mind if we zigzag through the middle decks? Check out where everything is?"

"Sounds good." Jake reached for Tommy's hand.

Cassandra paled as her gaze dropped to the boy she clearly hadn't connected to them.

"It's okay. I've got him," Sam reassured. When Jake hesitated, as he always did since losing his wife,

Sam added, "He's safe with me." His mind flashed to Jimmy, and he strained to swallow the lump that rose to his throat.

But Jake nodded as if he had no doubts, then led the way with Cassandra on his arm, leaving Sam and Tommy to trail behind. At least the woman was dressed in something more modest than the outfit she had on the other night.

The main lobby atrium, with its four-story ceiling and glass elevator, was even more crowded than when they'd boarded an hour ago. They took the spiral staircase to the next level, admiring the opulent crystal and brass fixtures, then rode the glass-walled elevator up another level to the promenade deck.

Tommy pressed his nose to the glass, entranced by the glittering lights.

"Ooh, I hear music. Let's go this way." Cassandra led them to an open lounge where a gifted musician played nostalgic tunes on a shiny baby grand.

Tommy tugged Sam toward brightly colored paintings lining the next hall. "Tommy and I are going to check out the art gallery." He'd already scoped it earlier, but another look wouldn't hurt.

"Sure, be right there. Be good for Uncle Sam, okay?" Jake called after them.

Sam wasn't convinced his brother had actually registered his own words. Not that Sam begrudged him the flattering attention of a beautiful woman. It'd been almost five years since Jake's wife had died. Sam just wished the woman wasn't one of his suspects.

Tommy tugged free of Sam's hold and veered toward the biggest and brightest painting—rainbow-colored air balloons floating in a pure blue sky—propped at floor level outside the gallery door. Along the way his foot caught the easel of another painting. Sam lunged to stop it from teetering over as Tommy skidded to a halt in front of the air balloons. "Look, Uncle Sam, there's a dog riding in the balloon!"

"Oh, we can't touch them," a kind voice singsonged. Jennifer Robbins. She squatted beside his nephew, her pleasant smile tempering the swiftness with which she'd caught his arm before he danced his grubby finger over the canvas. "They're beautiful, aren't they?"

Tommy bobbed his head up and down.

"Makes me wish I could ride in such a beautiful balloon."

The balloons weren't the only thing that looked beautiful. Sam almost hadn't recognized Jennifer with her blond curls spilling over her slender shoulders and wearing a casual, earthy-looking skirt and blouse that reminded him of commercials for romantic beach getaways.

"Do you like to draw?" she asked, and Tommy's head-bobbing grew more exaggerated.

Sam stepped behind him.

Jennifer glanced up, her warm smile turning to surprise. "Sam, hi!"

He placed a cautioning hand on Tommy's shoulder. "Sorry about that. He got away from me."

Her glance skittered to his left hand and back to his face. "This adorable little boy belongs to you?"

"He's my nephew, Tommy. Jake's son." The ease with which she interacted with Tommy stirred an unwelcome appreciation for the woman. Her sister had scarcely looked at the boy—a fact that would eventually cool Jake's interest, he was sure. "We were heading up to the buffet to meet my folks."

"Well, hi, Tommy! I'm Jen," she said then turned to Sam. "Let me see if the gallery has any coloring books and then I'll walk with you. I told my sister I'd meet her there."

"Yeah, we ran into her on deck." He hitched his thumb over his shoulder. "She and Jake stopped to listen to the piano player."

Jennifer frowned. "Tommy's mother isn't here?"

"She died when Tommy was an infant."

"Oh, I'm sorry." Sadness shadowed her eyes as she rose. "Let me get that coloring book."

As Jennifer spoke to the balding middle-aged man behind the counter, Sam took the opportunity to scan the gallery for the two contributions the Robbins sisters were to bring aboard for auction. Contributions that might also prove to be pivotal to his case. Cruise lines normally auctioned prints, not originals, and would ship a comparable one from their warehouse to the winning bidder, rather than the actual item displayed. The fact that the cruise line had agreed to ship the Robbins Gallery's actual contributions to the winning bidders, suggested they were originals, or if not, begged the question—was there more to the items than there appeared?

Jennifer knelt in front of Tommy and offered him a booklet of ship-themed coloring pictures and a package of four crayons. "For you."

Tommy grinned. Sam gave his shoulder a squeeze. "What do you say?"

"Thank you!" He threw his arms around Jennifer, who toppled back onto her behind then laughed at his exuberance.

Sam's heart squeezed uncomfortably at how good she was with the boy. He scooped Tommy into his arms then offered Jennifer a hand. "Sorry about that."

Laughter continued to brim in her eyes. "No need to apologize. That's the best hug I've had in a long time."

"How have you been? Did the police catch the jerk who vandalized your car?" Sam knew they hadn't, but he hoped his concern would win her confidence.

"No, but thankfully there haven't been any more incidents." She fussed with the delicate gold cross resting on a fine chain at her throat, and Sam wondered if the symbol actually meant something to her. She bit her bottom lip, looking way too vulnerable for his comfort.

She's a suspect, he reminded himself. Just because she got threatened didn't mean she wasn't guilty. Criminals threatened other criminals all the time. For all he knew, she was aware of who was behind the attack and couldn't identify him without revealing her own crimes.

"Except…" She let out a breath. "Last night some-one kept calling my apartment and not saying any-thing."

That wasn't good. "You tell the police? Try getting the number from the phone company?"

Her rejected grant applicant hadn't had an airtight alibi for the night of the attack, but without finger-prints or security video to connect him to the scene, the local PD hadn't been able to charge him.

"No, I just unplugged the phone." She offered a self-deprecating smile.

"That works, too." He didn't want to examine too closely why seeing that smile made him happy. She'd confided in him. It was a good start. His job was to gain her trust. Pure and simple. He set Tommy down as they stepped out of the gallery.

"Hold up a sec." The clerk hurried over and pressed a small note into Jennifer's hand. "The information you wanted."

"Thank you." She quickly tucked the note into her pocket before turning back to Sam.

Instinctively he knew the exchange had to be con-nected to his case. Another piece of the puzzle fall-ing into place. So why did he feel so disappointed?

Jennifer fingered the paper in her pocket, debating how to get away from Sam for a few minutes to make the call in private. She'd recognized the ship's cura-tor from the Seattle gallery where he used to work—one that had had a scandal he'd exposed, much to the owner's dismay. He'd seen right though her veiled questions about his experience and offered her the number of the PI he'd used.

Sam steered his nephew a wide berth around the art displays lining the hall. "I guess the art world's tight-knit?"

Reflexively Jen's hand crumpled the paper with the PI's number. "Pardon me?"

Sam motioned to the ship's gallery curator. "You all know each other."

"Oh, yes, he used to be at a Seattle gallery, but I'm not actually all that involved with the gallery, aside from attending the odd opening night for special exhibits." She glanced around at the ship's eclectic collection. There were few pastoral scenes like her mother's beloved early works. "My uncle insists I put in an appearance. Says it's bad for business if the owners don't show." Why was she telling Sam all this?

"Your uncle?"

"The gallery's curator. He's not really an uncle. He was our guardian after our parents died, so we call him Uncle." She bit her lip to stop her nervous rambling. She wasn't sure what had her more rattled— the idea of hiring a PI to spy on him while they were away, or the thought of what other illegal activities he might be up to. "Um… could you excuse me a minute? I need to make a phone call before I catch up with my sister."

"Go ahead. Tommy and I will browse for a few minutes."

Jennifer moved to the groupings of couches and

chairs on the other side of the wide hall opposite the specialty dining room next to the gallery and, turning toward the ship's windows, pulled out her cell phone.

The same sense of being watched that she'd felt outside the gallery last week shivered down her spine. Surreptitiously she scanned the wide hall and dining area beyond. A waiter in a crisp white shirt and black pants and vest approached. A linen napkin lay draped over his arm, and a glass of amber liquid on ice sat on his small round tray. He presented it to her with a slight bow.

"You have the wrong person. I didn't order a drink."

"It is complimentary," he said in broken English.

Jen glanced toward the bar, wondering if he meant someone had bought it for her, but she didn't see anyone looking her way. Her gaze skittered down the hall to the gallery where Sam stood with a cell phone pressed to his ear, frowning at the waiter. His attention jerked back to Tommy.

"Thank you," she said to the waiter without reaching for the glass. "But I don't drink."

"Not alcohol. Ginger ale," the waiter assured.

"Are you sure?"

He nodded.

She scanned the bar area again, but no one seemed ready to take credit for the offering. "Did someone buy this for me?" she enunciated each word slowly, hoping the waiter would understand.

He shook his head. "First day. First drink free."

The ice tinkling in the glass sure looked tempting. Everyone else sitting along the window seats held similar glasses. "Thank you." She accepted the drink and took a sip.

After a slight bow, the waiter withdrew.

Jennifer dialed the PI's number, but the call rolled immediately to voice mail. She waited a minute and tried again. Then a third time. She glanced at her watch. Five-thirty. They had two and a half hours before the ship left port and perhaps another hour after that before she lost cell phone reception. She'd try again later.

She stuffed her phone back in her purse and rejoined Sam and Tommy, who'd plopped himself on the floor and started coloring.

"Get ahold of who you were after?" Sam asked.

"Busy. I'll try again later. Ready to go?"

"First, what do you think of this piece?" Sam pointed to a Native American sculpture. "I've heard the artist's work is internationally sought after."

She shrugged. "Not really my taste."

"But for what it is, do you think it's a good value or overpriced?"

She eyed him speculatively. Men—the kind who were guaranteed to be wrong for her—inevitably tried to gain her attention by feigning an interest in art. That or they really were connoisseurs. Yet the curious sparkle in Sam's eyes didn't give away any hidden agenda. Then again, her track record for spotting them wasn't the best. She glanced at the four-figure ticket price. "I don't know what its market value is. Sorry."

He studied her intently then chuckled. "But you'd never pay that much for it."

She let a smile slip. "No, I wouldn't."

"Fair enough."

"Hey, you found her." Jake's voice boomed from behind them.

"Dad-eee," Tommy snatched up his coloring book and scurried into Jake's waiting arms.

Jake scooped him up in one smooth sweep, his face glowing with fatherly pride.

Cassie's complexion went pasty, but to her credit she didn't give away her discomfort in any other way. Jen hadn't been surprised that Cass had attached herself to someone aboard. She never could stand to be alone. Of course, now she'd probably want to hunt down someone more her type—not a man tied down by a child but someone wild and daring…a playboy. Definitely *not* the kind of guy Jen wanted to spend ten days around. And if Cass spent all her time flirting, Jen would never get the chance to broach the subject of selling the gallery.

"Can we eat now?" Tommy squealed.

"Sounds like a plan," Sam and Jake said in unison.

As they made their way down the hall, Jen admired the view through the ship's windows—clear blue skies, sunlight dancing on the choppy water, the odd sailboat gliding by. She misstepped, feeling as if the ship had dipped over a wave, but the ship wasn't moving yet.

Sam caught her elbow. "You okay?"

"Yes. I—" She swayed, and not just from the tingle

skittering up her arm at Sam's touch. "Whoa. Um, I guess I got a little dizzy looking at the water."

He held her steady. "Do you get seasick?"

"I don't know. I've never been on a ship. I put on a patch, just to be on the safe side." She tucked her hair behind her ear and pointed to the seasickness patch she'd put on last night—twenty-four hours before setting sail, like the directions had said.

Sam moved to her other side, between her and the window. "Maybe just focus on the hall for now, until you get your sea legs."

"Good idea." She tried not to think about how sweet Sam was being. Her sole mission this trip was to convince Cass to agree to sell her half of the gallery. Maybe one day, after their names stopped being synonymous with wealthy heiresses, she could trust a man's attention again.

They soon reached a bank of elevators and Cass hit the up button. The numbers above each door all hovered around fourteen. "Looks like everyone has the same idea about hitting the buffet," Jake said.

A group jostled past them, glanced up at the numbers and then climbed the spacious stairs. Jen hoped the men wouldn't suggest they do the same. She suddenly didn't feel so good.

They stepped on the first elevator that opened. It stopped one deck up, where a waiter stepped on— the waiter who'd served her the drink. He nodded then turned to the front. The elevator's movement made her brain feel like Jell-O jiggling in a bowl. She pressed her palm to her temple.

"You getting a migraine?" Cass's face swam in front of Jen's eyes.

"I don't know." Jen's muscles turned as jiggly as her brain. "I suddenly feel weird." Her head seemed to be floating. She felt her legs give way in a kind of detached, surreal way. As she was sinking, the lights went out. Strong arms came around her—solid, unwavering.

Cass called her name as if she were far away. A male voice, too. Sam's. But she kept sinking until she couldn't hear anymore.

THREE

"What's wrong with her?" Cass screamed.

Sam eased Jen gently to the elevator floor so he could check her airway, breathing and circulation. The ABCs of his first responder course spiraled through his mind like a CD on replay. "Jake, help me." He was the firefighter. He knew what to do. Jake knelt beside him, Tommy clinging to his neck.

The elevator doors opened.

"Gran—" Tommy squealed and lunged for his grandparents, who were standing at the door waiting to board.

Sam's mom quickly overcame her surprise at the sight of the slumped woman and wrapped Tommy in her arms.

"We've got to get this woman to sick bay," Jake said. "We'll meet you at the buffet when we can or back at the room."

"What deck is sick bay?" Sam asked the ship employee standing in front of the elevator panel.

"Oh, uh, Deck Five, Plaza," he said in a thick Eastern European accent.

"Well, hit it, will you?"

The man did as he was told, but the elevator stopped at the next deck down. "Excuse me. I get off here."

Cass lunged at the control panel and slapped the five again. "Is she going to be okay?"

"Her respiration is good. Pulse is rapid," Jake said. "Does she have any medical conditions or allergies?"

"No, not that I know of."

The elevator doors opened on the fifth floor and Sam swept Jen into his arms. She was impossibly light, as if a strong nor'easter could sweep her off the deck. His chest crunched at the unwelcome image.

"Which way to sick bay?" he asked the startled passengers waiting to board the elevator.

"Deck Four—Gala, one down—turn left," a woman spoke up.

Cass slapped the 4 button. "How could a ship employee not know where sick bay is? He told us five."

A few seconds later the doors pulled open again, and Sam charged left with Jen in his arms, Cassandra and Jake following.

A middle-aged woman in green scrubs directed him to lay her down on a bed, then she immediately checked Jen's vitals as they relayed what they knew.

The nurse pulled on reading glasses and jotted down Jen's blood pressure reading. "What has she had to eat or drink in the past three hours?"

Cassandra perched on a chair beside the bed and clutched Jen's hand. "Nothing that I know of." Black tears streamed down her cheeks. "We were on our way to supper."

"She had a glass of something a bit ago," Sam interjected. "I didn't see what."

The nurse eyed him suspiciously as she felt Jen's glands. Not that he blamed her. He was kicking himself for not intervening when he saw that waiter press a drink on Jen that she didn't seem to want.

The nurse's expression changed. She swept back Jen's hair and pulled off the seasickness patch. "Not sure if this is a contributing factor to her blacking out. But we've seen a number of negative reactions to these."

Cass gasped. "Is she going to be okay?"

The nurse patted Cass's shoulder. "Her respiration is a bit slow, but her vitals are good. We'll continue to monitor her until she comes to, unless you'd prefer we evacuate her to a hospital immediately."

"Do you think we should?"

"The doctor will be here shortly. Let's wait to see what he thinks."

"But that's what you think it is?" Sam asked. "Just the seasickness patch?"

"Did she take any recreational drugs? Alcohol?" The nurse's gaze narrowed in on Cass. "It's important you tell me everything so we can provide the best care to... This is your sister, right?"

"Yes. She doesn't do drugs." Fresh tears streamed down Cass's cheeks. "Or drink." Cass swiped at her damp face. "This is all my fault. She didn't even want to come on the cruise."

Jake rubbed Cass's back. "It's not your fault. She's going to be okay."

The nurse turned her attention to Sam. "You said she had a drink. What was it? Did she leave it unattended?"

"Can we speak outside a minute?" He cupped her elbow and steered her firmly out of the room. Once the door was closed he asked, "You think someone put a roofie in her drink?"

The nurse looked at him over the rim of her glasses. "And how do you know about Rohypnol?"

"C'mon, you just went through the list of what every woman shouldn't do if she doesn't want her drink spiked with a date rape drug."

Jake appeared at the doorway, listening in.

The nurse shrugged. "I can't verify it without a urine sample."

"But the symptoms fit?" His heart went back to racing a mile a minute. "Even if she only had the drink ten minutes before she passed out?" Sam knew why the nurse was being cagey. She wasn't at liberty to discuss a person's medical condition with a non-relative. But if he was going to catch whoever did this to Jen, he needed answers.

The nurse perched her reading glasses on her head. "Depending on the dose, roofies can take effect within minutes. Symptoms typically peak at two hours."

"How long before she wakes up?"

The nurse hesitated.

"How long is a patient typically out?" he rephrased impatiently.

"A few hours, at least." She glanced toward a couple of other occupied rooms and lowered her voice. "If you think she ingested the stuff less than an hour ago, the doctor will give her activated charcoal. It'll soak up the drug from her stomach and intestinal tract."

Sam inhaled. "And if I'm wrong?"

"If it's been longer than an hour since ingestion, or we're wrong about the substance, it'll be pretty useless, but it won't hurt."

"Good. In the meantime, I'll see if I can track down the source." He turned to Jake, still standing at the door to Jen's room. "You mind staying with them?"

"No problem. You go on."

Sam raced up the three flights to the lounge where Jen was given the drink. A balding, forty-something Caucasian man staffed the bar. The waitstaff was all female.

Sam stepped up to the bar.

"What can I get you?" the barkeep asked.

"I'm looking for the waiter who served the customers by the windows about forty-five minutes ago. Do you know where I can find him?"

"Him?" The bartender frowned and went back to polishing the glasses lining the bar. "Not sure who that'd be. My staff tonight are all women." His bar phone rang. "Excuse me," he said, reaching for the phone.

Great. So someone *impersonating* a waiter brought her a drink. That made the elimination process a whole lot tougher. He hadn't gotten a look at the guy's face, and Jen wasn't going to be in any condition to look at passenger photos any time soon.

Sam pictured the man he'd glimpsed from behind. As soon as the bartender finished his call, Sam said, "The guy I'm looking for was about five-ten, short dark hair, wore a black-and-white waitstaff uniform. Did a guy fitting the description order a soft drink from you?"

"You with the woman in sick bay?"

How'd he—? The phone call. The nurse must've notified security already. "Yes."

"I'm sorry. No men dressed like that ordered a drink from me." He waved over a waitress. "Hey, did a waiter-looking guy order a drink from you?"

"No, I would've remembered that." The woman laid her empty tray on the bar, along with an electronic cruise-card reader.

Although food was included in the cruise price, drinks weren't, which meant that if a passenger bought Kate the drink, his card would've been swiped. "Hey, can you get security back on the phone and ask them to look up everyone who paid for a soft drink—" Sam glanced at his watch "—between four and four-thirty? If they can line up the customers' photos, my friend should be able to identify the guy." And Sam wouldn't have to reveal he was FBI or that his interest in finding the guy went beyond a drugged drink.

"Sure thing. They'll be all over it."

Sam scratched his arm, his finger catching on a fine gold chain that was snagged on his sleeve. He carefully freed it, and a tiny cross slipped into his palm. Jen's. He stroked his thumb over the delicate etching, recalling how fragile she'd felt in his arms.

He clapped his hand closed and shoved the pendant into his pocket. "Jezebel" had pretended to believe in God to wile her way into his confidence. Wearing a cross didn't mean anything.

What he needed to know was who would want to knock Miss Robbins out? And why? And did the reason have anything to do with his investigation?

He needed to talk to her sister. He rode the elevator up to the Lido deck to grab some pizza slices for everyone first, then headed back to sick bay.

Outside Jen's room, Sam got an update on her condition The doctor felt certain she'd been drugged, but would be fine, and her sister had opted not to have her transported off the ship.

"Anything?" Jake asked as Sam rounded the corner.

Sam shook his head. The more he thought about it, the more he wondered if Jen could've been slipped the drug earlier because from what he'd seen, she'd only sipped whatever the waiter had brought her, and there'd been less than twenty minutes for it to take effect. Rohypnol was fast-acting, but…

He offered Cassandra a pizza slice. "I know the nurse asked you this before, but are you sure your sister didn't eat or drink anything else? Maybe stop for a coffee before you boarded? Take any medicine?"

"I don't know. We met at the pier and came straight aboard." Cassandra had wiped the mascara streaks from her face, but she still looked as if she'd gone through an emotional ringer. "There was a fruit and chocolate basket waiting for us in our room. She might have taken something from it."

"Do you mind if we go check?" He motioned to her plate. "After you've eaten. Knowing what your sister ate or drank might help the doctor speed her recovery."

Cassandra ate faster and asked Jake to stay with Jen in case she woke while they were gone.

Sam leaned over the bed and brushed a wisp of hair from Jen's cheek. She looked like Sleeping Beauty lying there, waiting for a handsome prince to awaken her with a kiss. His stomach fluttered at the thought and he quickly straightened. His hand knocked a crumpled paper on the bed. The note from the gallery curator?

Sam palmed the paper, stepped away from the bed and shoved his hand into his pocket. Taking a chair behind Cassandra's line of sight, he glanced at the paper. A phone number. Seattle area code with the name Watson. He pulled up the internet on his cell phone and looked it up. John Watson, private detective.

Why was his suspect calling a PI?

Too soon, Cassandra was ready to head up to her room. He feigned surprise when her room turned out to be next to his—an arrangement that had cost the bureau an extra three hundred bucks. Their carry-on luggage lay open on the bed. Their larger bags hadn't yet been delivered. Cassandra pointed to a large basket on the desk next to the balcony's sliding glass door. The plastic wrap and ribbons lay open beneath it. "Looks like Jen got into it, but—" Cassandra sifted through the contents "—I'm not sure what she had. The water bottles are missing, but she probably put them in the fridge."

Cass checked the small bar fridge in the opposite corner. "Yeah, there's only the two bottles that our steward left here and one from the basket."

Sam lifted an empty bottle from the trash can under the desk. "A raspberry-flavored water."

"She always drinks the raspberry. I hate it. Tastes too much like medicine."

"Who sent you the basket?"

"Oh." Cass flushed, apparently cluing in to the implication of his question. "Uh, Uncle Reg."

"And what flavor did your uncle include for you?"

"Blueberry."

Sam dropped the empty bottle into a plastic bag sitting on the desk, along with the unopened bottle.

Cass gave him a curious look. "What are you going to do with those?"

"Show the ingredients to the nurse." He had no means of testing it on the ship, but at the first port he could have it couriered to their Anchorage office or, better yet, he could send it back to Seattle with the pilot directing the ship out of the Sound.

He glanced at his watch. He probably had time to catch him. "Could you collect any medicines Jennifer might have taken?"

"You think there might have been some weird interaction?"

"It's a possibility." He examined the fruit and chocolate in the basket for signs of tampering.

"I had that happen to me once. Broke out in hives whenever I ate a banana within a couple of hours of my multivitamin." She dug through the night table drawer next to the bed and pulled out a box containing seasickness patches and a bottle of ibuprofen. "Switched vitamins and never got them again." She dumped her find into his bag.

"Do you mind if I check the bathroom?"

"Go ahead. She's particular about her moisturizers and shampoo and stuff. All scent-free. I don't think any of that would have reacted."

The bathroom barely had enough space to turn around in, let alone enough counter space to sort through her makeup bag. He carried it out and dumped the contents on the bed. Toothpaste, lip gloss, an assortment of lotions. Sam returned the contents to the bag. Any of the products could have been injected with a substance that soaked through the skin, but it was improbable. And she would not be happy if he unnecessarily confiscated them all.

The water was a likely source, but what motive would her uncle have for making her temporarily incapacitated at an unpredictable time of day or night?

Sam picked up the small card lying next to the basket on the desk. It wasn't signed. "How do you know the basket was from your uncle?"

Cass stood by the balcony door, looking out, and jumped at his question. "Uh, it said so on the card."

"No, it didn't." It merely said "Bon Voyage." He angled it her way.

She stared at it dumbly. "You're right." She sounded surprised. "I guess we just assumed since he gave us the cruise as a birthday gift. Who else would?"

"Either of you have a boyfriend?"

"I have lots of guy friends." Cass's cheeks reddened. "But I told your brother. Just so you know, I'm not leading him on or anything."

"Okay." Explained a lot. No wonder Jake had been enjoying her company so much—no strings. "Could any of your guy friends have sent this?"

She shrugged. "Maybe Uncle Reggie's son. Reg isn't really my uncle, of course."

Uncle or not, the idea that their long-time guardian would slip a roofie into Jen's drink was downright disturbing. "Let's get back to your sister. You might want to grab a sweater and a book. Could be a long night."

Sam escorted Cass back to sick bay, and Jake slipped out of the room as she took his seat next to Jen. "Find anything?"

"Maybe." Sam drew Jake deeper into the empty waiting room and lowered his voice. "I'm going to see if I can send these back to Seattle with the pilot.

Have them tested. Do you mind hanging around a while longer and keeping an eye on Cass and Jen?"

"Do you know why someone would do this to Jennifer?"

"No." Sam felt in his pocket for the PI's phone number, hoping it might offer some answers.

Jake narrowed his eyes. No doubt rethinking Sam's lame excuse for identifying himself as Sam Tate to the women the other night.

"I don't." Sam insisted. "Believe me. I wish I did."

Jennifer squeezed her eyes against the light seeping past her lashes. Her head felt ready to explode. And the bed…

Why was it rocking from side to side like a…*boat!*

She lurched up. "We're moving!" She clutched her head and dropped back to the mattress, rolled onto her side and curled her legs into her chest.

"Jen, what's wrong? Do you feel sick?" Cass's worried voice sounded above her ear.

"My head hurts," Jen moaned, trying to remember what she'd wanted to do before they left port. She massaged her fingers over her forehead, straining to coax out the memory, but she couldn't make sense of anything. Faces swam through her mind—Sam's, his sweet nephew's, a *waiter's?*

"Can you remember anything?"

Jen slit open an eye. "Where am I?" Why did her mouth taste so acidic?

"Sick bay. You passed out in the elevator when we were heading up for dinner. Sam carried you here."

Sam? This was the second time something bad had happened when he was nearby.

"What's the last thing you remember?" another female voice said.

Jen tilted her head to see who belonged to the voice—a woman in green scrubs. "Are you a doctor?"

"Nurse." She plugged a stethoscope into her ears and pressed the other end to Jen's chest. "We believe you were drugged."

Her heart lurched. "Drugged? How?"

The nurse placed two fingers at the pulse point on Jen's wrist and turned her attention to her watch. "That's what your friend's been trying to figure out."

"Sam," Cass filled in.

After another ten seconds or so, the nurse dropped Jen's wrist and recorded something on her chart. "You had a drink not long before you blacked out. Do you remember?"

Jen clutched her head tighter. "I knew I shouldn't have accepted it. I had this feeling. But the waiter said it was complimentary, and everyone seemed to have one."

The nurse rubbed Jen's shoulder consolingly. "Well, we've given you charcoal to absorb whatever might have been in the drink, and notified the ship's security. One of the officers will be here soon to talk to you."

"Does she need to stay here?" Cass asked.

"I'd like to continue to monitor her vitals through the night. If nothing changes, she can go back to her room in the morning." The nurse patted Jen's arm.

"But I'm afraid you'll likely have a lingering headache for a few days." She paused at the door. "Your fellow's out here pacing the hall, anxious to see you. Shall I let him back in?"

Unable to comprehend what the nurse meant, Jen flashed Cass a questioning look.

"She means Sam." Cass grinned. "He's really worried about you."

Something warm and soft filled Jen's chest at her sister's words. "Let me freshen up first." She sat up and the pain in her head exploded. As Cass helped her to her feet, Jen swayed, taking Cass sideways across the room in a zigzag toward the washroom.

"I'm so sorry," her sister whispered.

Jen stiffened, trying to make sense of the apology through her pain-filled fog.

"Here I talked you into coming on this cruise," Cass went on, "saying you'd be safer, and look what happened."

"This isn't your fault," Jen assured, except…who *was* to blame? Her limbs began to tremble. "Why would someone do this to me?"

"Some men are just sick." Cass waited for her to do her business then helped her back into bed and cracked open the room door. "You need to be on your guard."

Shivering, Jen closed her hand over the cut she'd gotten after that creep stabbed the note to her car. The police hadn't been able to prove it was Lester. Some stalker might've followed her onto the ship. "Do you think this is connected to the note in my car?"

"Do you?" Sam asked from the doorway.

The concerned timbre of his voice rumbled through her chest. Gripping the edge of the sheets, she pressed her arms against her rampaging heart. "I don't know. I don't know why anyone would do this to me." She closed her eyes, and when she opened them again, Sam hovered over her bed, deep grooves slashing his forehead. At the tender look in his eyes, her stomach cartwheeled. "Why...why do you care so much?"

He straightened abruptly, his Adam's apple bobbing. "I don't want to see you hurt."

Strangely, his sudden retreat endeared him to her more. Most guys would be quick to take advantage of her vulnerability.

"Sam talked to security about your previous attack so they'd check the passenger manifest," Cass said. "That Lester guy isn't on the ship. I think you just got targeted by some creep for no other reason than he's a creep."

Jen couldn't pull her gaze from Sam's. "Is that what you think?"

His brow creased with sympathy. "It happens. Can you remember anything that might help us figure out who did this?

"The waiter had an Eastern European accent."

Cass sprang to her feet. "Like the waiter in the elevator?"

Jen squeezed her eyes shut, trying to dig up the memory. She shook her head. "I don't remember being in an elevator."

"It's okay," Sam soothed. "But in case this wasn't a

random act, or the guy fears you'll identify him, it'd be better if you don't go anywhere alone."

"Are you volunteering to be her bodyguard?"

"Cass!" Jen gasped at her sister's brazenness.

Sam chuckled. "I'd be happy to escort you any time." The light dancing in his eyes reeled Jen in and spun her in dizzying pirouettes, leaving her breathless. She pressed her palm to her head. That drug had to be seriously affecting her brain. She did not let herself get swept up by guys she scarcely knew. Not anymore.

That was Cassie's department.

FOUR

The next morning, Sam phoned the FBI's Seattle office from the balcony of the room he shared with his brother and nephew. He couldn't make out what was going on in the twins' room next door any better from out here than he had with his ear to the wall inside as Jake and Tommy watched morning cartoons. And he doubted Jake had bought his neck-stretches excuse for hovering near the wall, no matter how lumpy the sofa bed looked.

"I put a rush on those bottles you sent in with the ship's pilot. Came back clean," the agent assured. "Couldn't find out who ordered the basket. Buyer paid cash. Not that it matters now, I guess."

Great, so they were back to square one. The PI had claimed he'd never heard of Jennifer Robbins. Not that Sam expected him to admit if he had. Not to some guy over the phone anyway.

"I spoke with the ship's captain," the agent went on. "Since their test confirmed Rohypnol in Miss Robbins's system, he'll get you the names of everyone who ordered soft drinks. But man, you might as well look for a needle in a haystack. We're talking hundreds of names."

Sam clenched the balcony rail, tamping down his frustration that Jen hadn't been able to pick out the waiter in the employee-photo lineup security showed her last night. "She told me that someone kept calling her the night before she boarded but didn't say anything. See if you can get a trace."

"You still think her spiked drink is connected to that note speared to her car last week?" the agent asked.

You'll pay. The note's threat had careened through his mind all night. Sam rammed the heel of his hand into the rail. "Yeah. Until we prove otherwise, I assume *everything's* connected."

The agent let out a low whistle. "If whoever drugged her planned to kidnap her and demand a ransom, he wouldn't have been able to stash her for long on a ship."

"Making a threat of 'pay now or you'll never see her again' all the more believable," Sam muttered, sideswiped by images of a bloated body washing ashore. How had this assignment veered so far off course? "Let me know if you find out anything else. Thanks."

He pocketed his phone and lifted his gaze to the horizon, where water met sky without a landmark in sight—kind of how this case felt at the moment.

Hearing a neighboring balcony door opening, he leaned over the rail to glance at the twins' balcony. One of the women stood with her back to the open door.

His own balcony door slid open and Sam jerked away from the rail as Jake poked out his head. "We're meeting Mom and Dad in the game room. Okay?"

"Uh, yeah." Sam's gaze strayed to the partition between the adjoining balconies. "I—"

Jake flicked his hand in the same direction. "Just knock on their door, why don't you? And invite them to join us."

"It's not what you think. I was just wondering how—"

Jake chuckled and retreated into the room. "Yeah, yeah, save your breath. We'll see you there."

Sam took his time securing their balcony door. This case was getting too messed up. He shouldn't be letting his family think his concern for Jennifer Robbins was personal. Not when the attacks were likely connected to the gallery's illegal activities.

Or she could be innocent.

Sam yanked open the door to the hall. They weren't innocent. He'd heard Cass on the wiretap confirm the appointment her uncle had arranged with the gallery owner in Skagway. He shut out the voice that reasoned that that didn't mean the women were guilty. He was *not* going to let a beautiful woman derail another case. He'd stick to Jennifer Robbins like a barnacle to a ship's hull, be a friend but strictly to do the job. Period.

As he lifted his hand to tap on their door, it opened.

"Oh," Cass exclaimed. "Good morning."

"Hey, I thought I'd check in on our patient."

"Thank you." Cass grabbed his arm and tugged him inside. "I'm going stir-crazy in this tiny room." She glanced over her shoulder to where Jennifer stood at the balcony door watching the water and lowered her voice. "I couldn't even get her to go out for breakfast. But when I ordered room service, she was too afraid to eat it. Said someone could've poisoned it. I have to get out." She wore black tights and a tank top and had her hair pulled into a high ponytail.

"You going for a jog around the deck?"

"Zumba class." She held up the ship's activity schedule. "It starts in five minutes. Could you please talk Jen into getting out of the room and enjoying the cruise?"

"Sure, you go on. I'll keep her company."

As Cass disappeared out the door, Jen turned from the balcony, startling at the sight of him. "How did you get in here?"

His heart kicked at the wobble in her voice. "Your sister let me in. I'm sorry, I didn't mean to frighten you." Even in a bright floral top she looked alarmingly pale. "My family's in the game room, and I wondered if you'd like to join us."

"Oh." Her breath left her in a whoosh. But whatever relief she'd felt at learning his intentions were honorable—at least honorable as far as she knew—was short-lived. "I...I better not." She stood by the open balcony door, cradling her middle.

He moved toward her but then thought better of

it. "Does your stomach hurt? Would you like me to take you to see the doctor?"

She dropped her hands to her sides and shook her head, and then as if she didn't know what to do, she scraped her thumbnail on the edge of the chair next to her. "I feel fine. Just…a little headache."

"Are you sure? Cass said you didn't eat."

Jen's gaze dropped to her thumb scraping back and forth. "Cass talks too much."

"You missed supper, too. You must be hungry," he said gently. "Eating might help with the headache."

She scooped an apple from the fruit bowl the steward had left on the desk. She rolled it between her fingers, scrutinizing the surface, then seemingly satisfied, she took a bite. "This is fine. I'm not a big breakfast eater." She was clearly trying to put on a brave front, but the deep shadows under her eyes and the defeated slump of her shoulders betrayed her. His heart went out to her—went out more than he wanted it to. More than was smart.

He stuffed his hands in his pockets to keep from reaching for hers. "C'mon and hang out with my family today. It'll take your mind off…last night."

"I can't even remember last night." She blinked rapidly as if staving off tears. "That's what scares me more than anything. Imagine what could have happened and I wouldn't have even known."

Yeah, that's all he'd been doing all night. "Hey." Despite his good intentions, he grazed his knuckles along her jawline. "We've got your back. Don't let this creep spoil your holiday, okay?"

Her eyes met his, appreciation brimming in their sparkling ocean depths. "You're right. Thank you. I'd love to meet the rest of your family."

Perfect. Maybe this assignment would be a cake-walk after all. If she was willing to hang out with them for the whole cruise and Jake sweet-talked her sister into joining them, he might not have to tail her on their Skagway excursion. She might invite them along.

He led the way to the game room, which was on the same deck as their rooms. Mom, Dad, Jake and Tommy sat near the windows at a large round oak table covered with dominoes.

Mom and Dad rose together and Mom clasped Jen's hands. "How are you feeling? We've been praying for you ever since we learned what happened."

"Thank you." Jen blinked again, her bottom lip quivering.

Sam wrapped an arm around her shoulders. "She's fine, Mom." The instant the words left his mouth, he wished he'd stayed the instinct to rescue Jen from his mother's inquisition.

Mom's gaze skittered from his arm on Jen's shoulder to his face, and a not-good pleasure lit her eyes.

He resisted the instinct to jerk his arm back to his side.

Dad extended his hand. "Pleased to meet you, Jen. I'm Sam's dad, Will Steele." He smiled at Mom as she loosened her hold on Jen. "My wife, Anne."

Jen's forehead furrowed. "Steele? I thought…"

She turned to Sam. "Didn't you say your last name was Tate?"

Dad's mouth flattened into a grim line. His parents knew better than to blow his cover, but the disappointment in Mom's eyes made him feel lower than dirt. This was supposed to be a special vacation. Not a job. The thought was written all over Mom's face.

Jake laughed. "He's always doing that. Doesn't think a woman will believe him if he tells her he's Sam Steele." Jake's foot pushed a chair into Sam's gut, letting him know he wasn't happy about what he'd just done for him.

Oh, yeah, he'd owe his brother big-time for his quick thinking.

Mom and Dad regained their seats, looking relieved by Jake's save.

Jen laughed. "Are you serious? People tease you about being a hard-boiled detective?"

"That was Sam Spade." Sam held out a chair for her. "But yeah, it's happened." To his parents he said, "Jen and her sister own the Robbins Art Gallery," hoping they'd assume he'd called himself Tate out of habit. He might do most of his undercover work on the East Coast, but the art world was too small to take chances.

"O-o-h." Mom patted Jen's hand. "I'm so sorry about your parents. I remember reading about their accident in the papers. You were much too young to lose them."

"Yes," Jen's voice cracked.

Sam steeled himself against a rush of sympathy he couldn't afford.

Tommy pressed a picture into her hands of a family waving from a boat with a bright yellow sun shining in the sky. "I drew this for you. To feel better."

Jennifer looked at the crayon drawing as if it were the most valuable piece of art she'd ever seen. "It's beautiful. Thank you." She pulled Tommy into a warm hug.

His nephew beamed under her attention.

Sam bumped his shoulder. "Good job, Bud."

Tommy slapped the table, sending the dominoes jumping. "Play it again, Sam?"

Jen smothered a giggle with her hand, her eyes twinkling, which got Mom started over Tommy's unintended Humphrey Bogart impersonation.

"See what I have to put up with?" Sam said.

Mom ribbed his arm. "Oh, you're so hard done by."

They flipped over all the dominoes and started a new game. Jen wasn't competitive at all. In fact, she seemed to go out of her way to set out pieces Tommy could use.

"Hey, if I draw you a pretty picture, will you help me, too?" Sam begged after Tommy laid a double combo, winning the game.

"Maybe." She flashed him an eye-twinkling grin, clearly enjoying the simple pleasure of playing a game with his family. Not something he would have expected.

Mom turned the played pieces over, mixing them

for a new game. "You're just out of practice. You need to get home more often."

"You don't live in the Seattle area?" Jen asked.

Did he imagine the hint of disappointment? He shook his head. She was a suspect. Their "relationship" wasn't going anywhere. "No, Boston."

"What do you do?"

Cringing at his family's collective breath, he said, "I'm in security." Experience had taught him to stick as close to the truth as possible, and given Jen's current trouble, he suspected she'd be more apt to trust someone in security than the art broker he usually posed as. "I've actually done a lot of work with art galleries."

"Look at the time," his mother jumped in. "That Iditarod racer is giving a slide presentation in ten minutes. I really wanted to hear that."

Jake started gathering dominoes. "Oh, yeah, about her sled dogs. You wanted to see that, didn't you, Tommy?"

"Yeah!" Tommy eagerly joined the cleanup, as Sam's dad sat back looking amused by his family's theatrics. A veteran police officer and sheriff, Dad likely hadn't doubted Sam could handle Jen's question. Not that Sam didn't appreciate his family's efforts to cover his back, except…more than once he'd infiltrated networks that wouldn't have just sliced *his* throat if they'd figured out he was an undercover cop; they'd have killed his family, too.

Another reason he preferred working on the opposite side of the country.

"Are you interested in seeing the presentation?" he asked Jennifer.

"Oh, yes, I think my sister mentioned that, too. I should leave a note in our room to let her know where I'll be."

"We'll save you seats," Mom chirped as they headed out.

"Beside me," Tommy squealed.

Sam couldn't blame his family for taking such a shine to her. But it was the gleam in his mother's eye that had him worried. That and Jen's wistful tone when she whispered close to his ear, "Your family's great."

They were. But they might not think the same about him after her arrest.

Leaving Sam in the hall, Jen crossed her cabin to the desk to jot a quick note for Cass. A smile tugged at her lips. Years ago, before the art gallery, she, Cass and their parents could while away an entire rainy afternoon playing games. *Thank you, Lord, for allowing us to cross paths with Sam and his family.*

A breeze whispered through her hair.

Jen's attention jerked to the open balcony door— then the closed bathroom door. "Cass, you back?"

No response.

The hair on Jen's neck prickled. Had she forgotten to close the door before she left? She reached to close it and glimpsed a man's shoe reflected in the wall mirror. "Sam!" she screamed.

Her intruder sprang from his hiding place and shoved her hard into the desk.

Sam rushed into the room just as the guy leaped onto the balcony rail and scrambled up a rope.

Sam grabbed his foot, but the guy caught Sam's chin with a wild kick, sending him reeling backward. Jen rushed to help him, but roaring his anger, Sam lunged for the guy a second time.

The guy shimmied out of sight, taking the rope with him.

Sam peered after him. "He climbed into the lifeboat suspended over the next deck up."

Jen raced back into the cabin and phoned security.

In minutes, the same security officer who'd questioned her last night showed up at her cabin door. As Sam relayed what happened, she looked in drawers and cupboards and suitcases to see what was missing. Trembling overtook her limbs. "Why was he here? What does he want?"

"Did you get a good look at him?" the officer asked. "Was it the same man who gave you the drink last night?"

"I don't know." She clenched her fists, refusing to fall apart in front of these men. "It happened too fast. And last night is too fuzzy to remember. But he had dark hair. I couldn't tell what color eyes. He was four, maybe six, inches taller than me. Wore brown leather shoes. And gloves. The surgical kind."

The officer relayed the description over his radio to men scouring the next deck. "Can you think of anything else? Clothes? Hair length?"

"He wore jeans," Sam said.

"Short hair," Jen added.

"Okay, my men are checking security footage now. Hopefully we'll be able to pinpoint who this guy is. What did he take?"

"Noth—" Jen swallowed to clear the catch in her throat. "Nothing that I can see. The safe hasn't been opened."

"What do you think he was after?" Sam asked.

"I don't know!" She ducked her head and chewed on her bottom lip, embarrassed at her outburst. "Cass and I don't have any more valuables in here than anyone else would."

"But given last night's incident, this doesn't feel like a random robbery." The officer clicked his pen. "Did you recognize any names on the list?"

"What list?"

The officer shifted his attention back to Sam. "We sent it to your room this morning. Didn't you get it?"

She stared at the list—three columns long—and gulped.

"You recognize any of the names?" the officer asked.

Jen sank onto the bed, the paper shaking in her hand.

Sam hunkered beside her and rested his hand on her forearm. His warmth seeped into her chilled bones and stilled her trembling. She darted him a grateful glance, but his attention was fixed on the page.

The names were listed alphabetically. By the time

she reached the Ps, she shook her head. "I don't know any of these people."

Sam's brow furrowed. "You know at least one."

FIVE

Her heart galloping, Jen's gaze veered back to the list of people who'd bought sodas last night. How did Sam know who she knew?

When she reached the Rs, her throat clogged. *Robbins*. "She wouldn't," Jen whispered even as Cass's *I'm sorry* streaked through her mind. "She wouldn't," Jen repeated, glancing uncertainly around their small cabin.

Sam nodded but didn't look convinced. He folded the paper and returned it to the envelope. "It could be a coincidence. But sometimes we don't know people as well as we think we do."

Yeah. She knew all about that. She'd never have believed her uncle Reggie capable of brokering stolen art, or of Ian only pretending to love her to get his greedy hands on her family's estate. But not Cass. Cass was her sister, her twin. "My sister would never do anything to hurt me."

"Well, she's clearly not your cat burglar," the security officer conceded. "We'll let you know as—" He stopped midsentence to answer his radio. "Copy that. I'm afraid your prowler was cleverer than we thought. The cameras that would have picked up his movements had all been re-angled."

He tipped his notebook closed. "I'm sorry. There's little else we can do unless you recognize the man. Be vigilant about using the security bar on the balcony door. Watch your drinks, and you probably shouldn't walk out on the decks alone."

A cold shiver rattled through her.

Sam squeezed her hand. "We'll watch out for you."

Only that's what he'd said this morning, and someone had gotten into her room. And she had no idea who. Or why.

By the time she and Sam finally got to the Iditarod presentation, it was wrapping up. Cass had already joined Sam's family, who'd intercepted her on their way. By mutual agreement, Jen and Sam didn't mention the break-in, not wanting to frighten Tommy or worry his parents. From the sparkle in his mom's eyes, she clearly had other suspicions of what had delayed them.

They had lunch together in the Bordeaux dining room, which felt like an exclusive five-star restaurant with its rich mahogany décor, pristine linen and incomparable ocean views. After missing last night's supper and breakfast this morning, Jen savored every bite of the delicious grilled chicken.

By the time they finished lunch, Jen had managed to push the break-in and Sam's suspicions of Cass to the back of her mind. At least until an announcement sounded over the ship's PA, reminding passengers of the art auction beginning in twenty minutes.

Sam's dad folded his napkin and set it beside his place. "I guess you two will want to check that out."

"Oh, absolutely," Cass gushed. "A couple of our gallery's numbered prints are in it. I love watching to see which pieces appeal to people and what they're willing to pay for them."

Jennifer muffled a groan. Sitting through an art auction was the last thing she wanted to do. But her whole reason for agreeing to the cruise was to have time alone with Cass, away from Uncle Reggie's influence, so she could convince her to agree to sell the company. And if Sam was right about the drink and the break-in and the note back in Seattle all being connected, they had to have something to do with Uncle Reggie's dealings—something else she should have the PI look into. Which reminded her…

She slipped her hand into her skirt pocket in search of the note with the PI's number. She hated to think what Uncle Reggie might have already gotten up to since she'd boarded the ship. Because he was paying for their room, she couldn't exactly make a ship-to-shore call without inviting questions, and her cell phone was useless this far from land. She'd have to buy some internet time and try contacting the PI that way. She dug around in her pocket until she noticed Sam eyeing her curiously.

She returned her hand to the table. Didn't matter anyway. The paper wasn't there. Now she'd have to sneak back to the gallery and ask for the number again. Not an easy thing, considering that between Cass and Sam, they were determined she shouldn't be left alone.

Maybe stopping by the art auction wasn't such a bad idea after all. It would be the perfect cover to ask the curator a *casual* question.

"I think I'll take Tommy to the pool," Jake said. "What do you say, Bud?"

"Yay!" Tommy bounced in his chair. "You coming, too, Uncle Sam?"

"A little later." He patted his stomach. "I'd sink if I went right now."

Tommy giggled and Jennifer couldn't help but smile over the sweet exchange.

The corners of Sam's eyes crinkled as he met her gaze, sharing her amusement. "I wouldn't mind tagging along with you and Cass for a bit, hone my art knowledge."

"We'd love for you to come." Cassie googled her eyes at Jennifer. "Wouldn't we?"

Everything in Jen instantly reared. Too many guys had befriended her for nothing more than her money or her connections or both. She'd vowed to never be so blinded again. And here she'd already lowered her guard around Sam. What made her think he was any different?

Every other guy had been really good at hiding his true intentions, too.

"Jen…" Cass pressed.

Jen pasted on a smile. The man lived on the other side of the country. That alone should convince her he had no insidious motives except to be nice and maybe a tad protective. "Sure! Let's go."

Once in the dimly lit lounge, as they waited for the auction to begin, Sam asked about the pieces their gallery had contributed—the artists, their provenance, what prompted their uncle to acquire them. The kind of questions that cooled her interest in a guy faster than anything.

At her sister's animated explanations, Jen's heart sank. She'd always thought Cass liked the work at the gallery only for the eligible bachelors and exclusive party invitations it brought. She'd never heard her talk about the art itself with such passion.

Jen was so tired of dodging the paparazzi, thanks to Seattle's insatiable interest in their twin heiresses—attention Cass seemed to thrive on. Attention that Jen honestly thought Cass would be better off getting away from, even before learning about Reggie's sideline. But was she being selfish?

She wanted a new start in a quiet town where people didn't care who her parents were or what size her bank account was. *Lord, I don't know what I'll do if Cass refuses to sell.*

Cass suddenly stopped her explanation. "I'm parched. Sam, would you mind getting me a soda?"

"Happy to." Sam pushed his chair back from the table. "Jen, would you like something?"

"Just water, thanks."

To Sam's credit, he went directly to the bar and watched the drinks get poured.

"What's wrong with you?" Cass blurted the instant Sam was out of earshot.

"What are you talking about?"

"Sam joined us because he clearly wants to spend time with you and you're totally ignoring him."

"I am not." She darted a glance toward him. *Not really.* "I just don't appreciate guys trying to impress me with their art knowledge."

Cass rolled her eyes. "Ever occur to you that he might just be trying to share your interests?"

Jen leaned across the table. "I'm. Not. Interested. In. Art."

"So tell him. Jen, he's a nice guy. Don't blow this because of that idiot Ian."

"There's no *this.*"

Sam watched Jen storm from their table, weaving around the lounge's half-moon tables flanked by leather armchairs to the makeshift stage. She browsed the eclectic mix of muted still lifes, lush landscapes and brightly colored abstracts, then stopped at the side of an easel where the curator was straightening a painting of a pigtailed girl running through a meadow of daisies. One of her mother's paintings, if Sam wasn't mistaken. One Cass had failed to mention.

A pained expression crossed Jen's face as she studied the picture.

Cass sat at the table, grimacing at her sister.

Besides wanting to safeguard Jen from whoever she'd surprised in their cabin, he'd horned in on their auction date because he'd been worried that Cass had "needed" to get out of her room this morning for some reason other than a Zumba class. Their gallery had supplied at least two pieces for the onboard auction. Pieces that he suspected might be masking another illegal sale—a sale for which Cass may have needed her sister temporarily out of the way in order to finalize.

A sale Jen may have just clued in to.

Except if Jen had been in the dark, why had she been the one trying to discourage him from joining them?

His heart fell at another possibility—that Jen didn't report anything missing because the prowler took what they'd smuggled aboard.

Jen spoke to the curator, who nodded and then skirted out of sight.

Sam delivered Cass's soft drink to their table, then hurried over to Jen for a closer look at the piece. "What do you like about this one?" He handed over her glass of water and edged nonchalantly around the painting to glimpse the back.

Clean brown wrapping paper hid the back from frame edge to frame edge.

He glanced down the row of items. Only one other back was masked in the same fashion. The cards on the front of the easels confirmed they came from the Robbins Gallery.

The cruise director motioned to them. "Please take your seats."

"It reminds me of my childhood," Jen said as they reached the table.

"Pardon me?"

"You asked me what I like about the painting." Her voice was surprisingly wistful considering the distress he'd seen on her face a few moments ago.

"It's one of our mom's early pieces." Cass leaned back in her chair, looking bored. "What Uncle Reggie calls sofa art. But it usually goes over well on the cruise ships."

"I like it better than Mom's later stuff," Jen said.

So did he. But to pull off his undercover assignments, he'd spent a great deal of time learning how to articulate a piece's merits or shortcomings, so he understood their uncle's mentality. Artists were valued for their ability to open the viewer's eyes to something deeper than a photographic reproduction of a scene. Apparently, Reginald Michaels failed to see the delight in simple pleasures shining in the young girl's eyes in the painting.

"My parents have a similar print in their den," Sam said, trying to gauge if it had merely been the mom connection that had elicited Jen's earlier frown. He leaned close and whispered, "When I was a kid, I had a crush on the girl. Is it you?"

Jen's face turned pink and he grinned. "I'll take that as a yes."

The unintelligible babble of rising bid values made further discussion difficult, which was a good thing because he had no idea what had possessed him to admit to that last part. He wasn't the kind of guy who'd lead a woman on more than necessary for the operation to succeed. He sat back and monitored the direction of Cass's and Jen's attention.

"Is that one of ours?" Jen asked as the auctioneer opened bids on a new piece.

"Yeah." Cass straightened, glanced at a gray-haired man who appeared prepared to lift his number.

Sam lifted his drink to his lips. Did he imagine Cass's slight headshake before her attention returned to the auctioneer? Maybe telling the old man this wasn't the piece he wanted?

The piece was set aside when no one accepted the opening price. *Curious.*

A waiter collected Cass's empty glass, and as he circled the table, Jen covered her glass with her palm. "I'm good, thank you."

The waiter slipped a business card beneath her coaster, his gaze flicking in the curator's direction.

Jen's lips formed a small "o" as she slipped the card into her pocket without looking at it.

Was this what she'd talked to the curator about? Something to do with the auction or maybe she was asking for that PI number she'd lost last night. He should've returned it to her, would've been a good excuse to ask about it. Maybe still would be…sometime when Cass wasn't around.

Sam pushed back his chair until their arms touched. "Aren't you going to read it?"

The "what?" that sprang to her lips died the instant she met his gaze. She had amazingly expressive eyes. The light from the small lamp on their table danced in them like sunlight on a sparkling lake. He'd tried to make the question sound casual, but her gaze dropped to his fingers clenched around the armrest, his muscles like tightly spun coils ready to erupt into action at her word. He shot a cold look at the waiter's retreating back so there'd be no mistake whose side he was on.

"It's just info I asked the curator for." She patted his hand. "Nothing to—" Her pupils dilated as if she'd felt the jolt that zinged up his arm at her touch, too. Wow.

He wasn't sure how long they stared at each other, but it was long enough for her sister to notice.

Cassie's chuckle jerked their attention back to the table. "I guess you guys have seen enough."

"No!" Jen blurted. "I—" She twisted her glass in the condensation pooling beneath it. "Cass, if you could do anything you want, what would you do?"

Cass made a shooing motion with her hands. "It's okay. Go swim with Jake and Tommy. I'll be up in a bit."

"No, no. That's not what I meant. I mean for a living. What would you do for a living? Where would you live?"

Cass's head tilted and twin lines appeared between her brows. "What are you talking about?"

Jen let out a muffled sigh, and Sam wondered along with Cass.

"I mean, our future will soon be ours to choose, not Uncle Reggie's. You must dream of things you want to do?"

Cass frowned and shrugged "Not really. I love working at the gallery."

"But you like to travel." Desperation crept into Jen's voice. "You could take a job that would let you see the world." She motioned to the man at the podium. "Like a cruise director. You'd be great at that."

Cass burst out laughing. "You've got to be kidding. Living at work 24-7 is not my kind of job."

"What about you, Jen?" Sam tilted his head, capturing her gaze. "What's your dream?"

"Oh, you know." She swept her arm through the air theatrically. "A husband who adores me, two-point-two kids and the house with a white picket fence." She ducked her head and traced the condensation dribbling down her glass, but he didn't miss the smile that tugged at the corners of her mouth.

"You'd prefer a house in the country, I imagine?"

Her smile broke loose, unleashing his own. He'd had the same dream once upon a time—his kids playing cops and robbers with his brother's and cousin's kids, just like they'd grown up doing. He shut down the thought.

"Yes." Jen's expression turned wistful again. "A place where everyone looks out for their neighbor and no one's looking to use you to climb whatever social ladder they're eyeing."

He leaned back, slinging his arm over his chair. "Sound's like there's a story behind that."

Her fingers traced her neckline, as if probing for something to grasp, then soon fell away. Her gaze drifted back to the painting of the child in the meadow. "Maybe I'll tell it to you sometime."

"I'd like that."

She squirmed, suddenly looking very uncomfortable.

The auctioneer had the stagehand bring Jen's mom's piece forward.

"I wouldn't mind bidding on the girl in the meadow," Sam said, hoping their reactions might betray whether they had other plans for the signed, numbered print. "How high do you think I should go?"

"Oh, no," Cass jumped in. "You don't have to bid here. We can give you a good deal on a print when we get back to Seattle."

"That's okay. I don't expect any special treatment." He pulled the paperwork explaining how to bid from the table's center to see if he needed to grab a number or if he could simply raise his hand.

Cass tugged the papers back. "I insist."

"Maybe he wants the fun of bidding," Jen argued, earning a glare from Cass. "I'm just saying."

Cass's gaze veered to the gray-haired man again.

Pretending to check his cell phone screen for the time, Sam snapped the man's photo and one of the painting. The FBI preferred he negotiated a price ahead of time when making a buy, and they wanted to know it was a sure thing, not a hunch that something more valuable lay behind it.

He tapped his foot, debating what to do, as Cass's apparent contact accepted the opening price. Sam raised his hand as the auctioneer upped the bid by twenty-five dollars. The other guy immediately out-bid that. Grateful he'd brought the field office's new compact satellite phone, Sam sent the images to his handler with a question mark and raised the bid.

The man scowled at Cass, then Sam, probably thinking he was a plant to force the bids higher. As the auctioneer called, "Going once," Cass's contact lifted his number to reclaim the highest bid.

Sam moved to make a counterbid, but Cass slapped her hand over his arm, her sharp nails scraping his skin. "Please, Sam, don't."

SIX

"What was that about?" Jen demanded the instant she and Cass returned to the privacy of their room.

Cass flopped on the bed. "Like I told Sam, I met the man in the gallery on my way back from the gym. He knew I was selling it. And here Sam's sitting right beside me, driving up the price. Imagine how that looked!"

Jen squinted at Cass, no more certain now she believed her story that the man bought it for his wife's birthday than she had been an hour ago.

"Of course…" Cass stretched the word out playfully. "I also wanted to give Sam an excuse to visit the gallery after we return to Seattle. Anyone with two eyes can see he likes you."

Jen's heart did a crazy jig. She crossed her arms to make it stop. "He lives in Boston."

Cass shrugged. "People move. They just need the right motivation. And don't tell me you're not interested in him, too. You were absolutely twitterpated when the two of you showed up an hour late for the Iditarod slide show."

Jen let out a horrified cough. Was that what his parents had thought, too? "I was upset, not *twitter-pated.* Our cabin had just been broken into!"

Cass snorted. "Yeah, right."

Jen planted her hands on her hips. "Didn't you wonder why Sam just checked out the room before leaving us?"

"I thought—" Cass levered to a sitting position. "I figured he was being extra careful because of last night. You're serious?"

"Yes. I didn't want to say anything in front of Tommy, and by the time we got to the gallery, I'd managed to put it out of my mind."

Cass sprang from the bed and rummaged through her suitcases, then checked the safe. "I'm not missing anything. Are you?"

"No."

She pulled a handful of socks from a drawer and dug around inside. "Are you sure it wasn't just the room steward?"

"The guy shoved me and escaped up the balcony by a rope!"

Cass dropped the socks, her face pale. "The same guy as last night?"

Jen sank onto the bed. "I don't know."

"What are we going to do?" Cass sounded genuinely panicked.

"Do you know what this guy could be after?"

"No!"

Jen let out a breath. Not that she'd expected Cass to say "yes" even if she did know. Part of her wanted to get off at tomorrow's port and fly home, but maybe that's what the guy wanted. And she hadn't even broached the subject of selling the gallery with Cass yet. Which, if this afternoon's conversation was any indication, wasn't going to be an easy sale.

"Well, then, maybe now he's figured out that we don't have anything worth bothering us about." She hoped.

"Why do I have to wear a tie? We going to a wedding?" Tommy complained, winding the tie his father had handed him around his head instead of his neck.

Sam knelt in front of his nephew and took over tying duty. "No, it's just a formal dinner. It'll be worth it. You'll see. You can have steak or chicken or pasta and—"

"I'd rather have hot dogs. I could have stayed in my swimsuit."

Jake laughed. "He's got you there, bro."

"Jennifer is joining us," Sam bribed, knowing his nephew had taken a shine to her.

Jake's laughter died on his lips. "Maybe this isn't a good idea." Since hearing about the break-in, he'd been more worried about Tommy's safety than ever. And Sam's grilling him over whether he saw Cass actually consume the drink she'd ordered last night hadn't helped, especially when Jake couldn't even remember her ordering it. Not that Sam was any more comfortable with the situation. Not since Cassie's sudden plea at the art auction.

Tommy made a choking sound. "Too tight!"

"Sorry." Sam eased off on the knot. "There, you're all set. Go grab your jacket."

"What exactly are these women involved in?" Jake growled.

"I don't know." And that truth worried him more than what he did know.

Jake drilled him with a look that could strip paint. "You know I won't stand by and do nothing if one of them is in trouble, but…I won't endanger Tommy."

"Neither would I," Sam hissed. "I'm telling you the truth. I don't know who's behind the attacks or why they are happening."

"But they're connected to something you're investigating." It wasn't a question. When Sam didn't respond, Jake shook his head in disgust. "I can't believe I thought you bought this trip just to get out of a party with the aunts and uncles and cousins."

Sam jolted at the admission, but he shouldn't be surprised. He hadn't been to a family get-together since… "We'd better go." He grabbed the necklace he'd forgotten to return to Jen. As he slipped it into his tux pocket, his thumb traced the lines of the cross, reminding him of the last cross-wearing woman he'd taken to dinner.

He squelched the thought. This situation was completely different.

He was the one looking for information. And he already knew Jen was trouble.

Cass joined them in the hall wearing a low-cut number Sam had seen in a photo of her at a gallery opening. Thankfully, for Mom and Dad's sake, not to mention Tommy's, the dress's neckline didn't plunge as low as others he'd seen. Her arrival seemed to improve Jake's mood.

"Jen ready?" Sam asked.

"Yes." Jen rushed out of the cabin in a swish of shimmering emerald—a color that did amazing things for her eyes. "Sorry to keep you waiting." She frowned and glanced down at her gown, smoothing the already perfect waistline. "Is something wrong?"

Jake slapped Sam on the back. "He's just speechless. You look stunning, Jen."

"Oh." She ducked her head, color staining her cheeks.

Sam tucked her hand through the crook of his arm. The feel of her delicate fingers elicited a wave of protectiveness *not* befitting a suspect. But considering how last night had turned out, he wasn't about to ignore it—or let her out of his sight. "You do look beautiful," he whispered close to her ear, her flowery fragrance filling his senses.

"You look pretty amazing yourself, Mr. Steele." Her husky pronouncement of his name rivaled that of "Mr. Bond."

"Why, thank you." He straightened his bow tie and mentally congratulated himself on remembering to pack his tux. Noticing her bare neck, he reached into his pocket and produced her necklace. "Have you been missing this?"

"Oh, Sam. Where did you find it? I was afraid I'd lost it." She lifted her hair. "Could you put it on?"

"I'm sorry I forgot to return it earlier." He unfas-

tened the clasp and slipped the delicate chain about
her neck. "I found it snagged on my shirt. It must've
happened when I carried you to sick bay last night."

Her silky hair spilled over his hands as she abruptly
turned. "You carried me? All the way to sick bay?"

He couldn't decide if she was horrified, pleased or
just embarrassed. He grinned. "It was no hardship.
Trust me." He got a kick of pleasure at how easily
she blushed.

"Are you two coming?" Jake called over his shoulder.

Sam tucked Jen's arm through his once again, and
they trailed Cass, Jake and Tommy down the hall. "I
guess the necklace is pretty special to you."

She fingered the cross. "It was my grandmother's."

"Ah." Special due to sentimental value more than
conviction. The thought bothered him more than it
should.

"Except I never really appreciated it until I came
to know the Lord for myself a few years ago. Do you
go to church?"

His heart skipped like a teenager's on the receiving end of a glance from the cutest girl in class. "Yes,
my faith is very important to me," he said, although
part of him had been tempted to say no. She seemed
like the kind of person who'd want to try and save
him. And Lord help him, he wanted to know if the
impression was true.

"I'm so glad to hear that." Jen cupped her hand
over their interlocked arms. "When your mother said

they'd been praying for me after what happened last night, I'd wondered."

Her response stirred warm feelings he had no business having. Oh, man, he needed to get out more.

"Where's Gran and Gramps?" Tommy tugged on Jake's suit jacket, and Jennifer frowned at her sister's obvious irritation.

Jake recaptured Tommy's hand. "They're meeting us in the atrium. They wanted to check out the captain's welcome-aboard party."

All their rooms were on the Emerald deck, which also happened to be the top floor of the four-story open atrium in the middle of the ship. A crowd waited at the glass-enclosed elevators to travel down the three floors to the dining room.

"Let's take the stairs," Cass suggested.

The marble stairs were wide with glittering gold handrails and wound down to the main floor landing where a tall pyramid of full champagne glasses waited for the taking.

Jen gasped, her arm tightening around Sam's.

"What's the matter?"

She pointed toward the white baby grand on the side landing two floors down. "That's the waiter who brought me the drink!"

Sam's attention jerked from the piano to the servers, but he couldn't see any waiter. In their dark suits or tuxes, most of the men looked the same. "Where?"

She hurried down three steps, then scanned the crowds. "He's gone."

"Are you sure it was him?" Cass asked.

"He looked right at me! And when he saw me notice him, he ducked out of sight." She was trembling.

Sam tucked her closer to his side and exchanged a look with Jake. If they had some idea what this guy wanted, at least they'd know what they were up against. What *he* was up against, Sam corrected himself. He couldn't ask Jake to help with protection details. He had Tommy to protect.

"There you are!" Sam's mom hurried toward them and whirled her arm at the well-dressed crowd greeting the captain and his crew. "Isn't it marvelous?"

With the chandeliers and shiny marble floors and all the glass or gold surfaces in between, not to mention the shimmering gowns on the ladies, the wide-open area resembled a glittering crowd under a spinning disco ball. Not an easy place to spot a guy who didn't want to be spotted.

Gramps took Tommy from Jake.

"Don't you look handsome?" he said to his grandson.

Tommy tugged at his tie. "Can we eat now?"

The laughing response was muted in all but Sam's parents, but there was no point in mentioning the sighting to them.

"Eating sounds good to me," Jen said, although Sam sensed she'd strained to inject the bright note into her voice.

Cass and Jake eyed her speculatively. Sam squeezed her hand, admiring her brave front.

Since they'd chosen the "any time" dining option, once in the dining room, the maître d' gave their group a table to themselves. Sam took a seat opposite Jake so that between them they could keep an eye on every waiter in the place. If someone wanted to poison someone, a ship was too easy a place to get away with it. Meals and drinks passed through so many hands, there was little hope of guaranteeing they hadn't been tainted.

From the way Jen picked at her salad, she must've drawn the same conclusion.

He leaned close to her ear. "Let's switch."

She gave him a startled look. "What?"

He took her salad bowl and slipped his into its place. "Okay?"

Her grateful look reassured him he'd made the right call, and he tacked on his own addendum to his Dad's prayer—that the food wouldn't make them sick.

Sam hadn't thought to order the same thing as Jen in time, so when the main course was served, she received grilled Alaskan salmon while he got a T-bone steak. "You want to switch?" he asked.

Her long lashes dropped sheepishly. "Do you mind?"

Yes! His mouth had been watering for steak since the second he'd walked into the dining room and smelled it. "Of course not," he lied. Well, not a total lie. He liked salmon, too. It just wasn't what he'd been craving.

They made the switch while Jake regaled Mom with a story of one of Tommy's antics. But their father noticed and lifted a questioning eyebrow. Sam just shrugged, which seemed to amuse him.

"So which shore excursion are you girls booked to go on tomorrow in Juneau?" Mom asked.

Jen looked to Cass. "Are we booked for a shore excursion?"

Sam bit back the answer, surprised he knew more about her itinerary than Jen. Of course, that was his job.

"Yes, we're going on the Mendenhall Glacier Float Trip, shooting rapids." Cass grinned.

"We are?" Jen didn't sound too keen on the idea.

"Hey, we're booked on that, too!" Jake shot Sam a sarcastic *imagine-that* look.

"You'll love it," Sam assured. "The rapids are gentle and you'll get magnificent views of the glacier."

"Is Tommy going?" Her tone implied she might believe him if his little nephew could handle it.

"No." Mom dabbed her mouth with a napkin. "He's coming with us to try his hand at dogsledding."

"Yeah," Tommy joined in. "Maybe they'll let me bring home a puppy like the lady showed in her pictures this morning."

Jake ruffled the boy's hair. "Not happening, Bud. You just enjoy them while you're there, okay?"

Tommy grumbled and squirmed in that you-can't-blame-a-kid-for-trying kind of way.

"That sounds more my speed," Jen said.

"The tour's already at capacity," Sam improvised. "That's why Jake and I opted for the raft tour."

"C'mon," Cass cajoled. "It'll be fun. The tour guides are professionals. They know what they're doing."

"That's what you said the last time you conned me into a rafting trip."

Sam washed down his salmon with a gulp of water. "What last time?"

"To celebrate high school graduation," Cass explained. "The raft capsized and she hasn't been on the water since. Until now."

Jen stopped sawing her steak and pointed her knife at Cass. "I almost drowned!"

"I didn't hear you complaining when Doug Roberts pulled you out and revived you with mouth-to-mouth."

Jen rolled her eyes, and a most becoming blush splashed onto her cheeks.

Sam's gut tightened. Something about how easily she blushed suggested an innocence that didn't jive with the facts of this case.

"Don't worry. As a fireman, I'm trained for any kind of rescue that might be needed." Jake's lips twitched into a crooked smile. "Including AR."

"Over my dead body," Sam growled, only half in jest, knowing his brother was baiting him to stake his claim.

Jen's eyes widened, and Sam hadn't thought it possible, but her face grew two shades darker. And he kind of liked it.

Mom patted Jen's hand. "Ignore them."

Sam switched dessert plates with her, settling for *crème brûlée* instead of NY cheesecake. "You can count on us to keep you safe. Okay?" If he'd been smart, he'd have told her to order the cheesecake and he could've ordered her *brûlée*.

Her appreciative smile made the sacrifice worth it, though. Almost. He swallowed a rush of bile. Not because he suspected any of the food had been tainted. But because he loathed custard. He glanced longingly at the chocolate brownie her sister had ordered and wished the twins shared the same taste in dessert. He pushed the *brûlée* away.

Jen slid the cheesecake back to him with only a forkful missing. "Enjoy."

Oh, yeah. He was really starting to like this woman.

The cheesecake turned to sawdust in his mouth. Wooing her for information was starting to feel a whole lot like betrayal.

"Go. You'll have fun," Jen's sister said from the bathroom—the room she'd occupied almost exclusively for the past three hours. "Take lots of pictures of the glacier for me."

"But I don't want to go without you," Jen said through the door. "I can't leave you like this."

Cass moaned. "There's nothing you can do. No point in both our days being ruined."

"Let me take you to the clinic."

"And be quarantined? No, thanks. I'm sure it's just a reaction to something I ate."

Jen's stomach roiled. What if Cass had been poisoned? Was Sam incapacitated, too, thanks to switching meals with her? She rushed to the phone to dial his room. She'd feel awful if he got sick after being so sweet.

A knock sounded at the door.

"Just a minute," she called, thinking it might be the steward. She peeked through the peephole, and at the sight of Sam standing there looking perfectly healthy, she yanked open the door. "You're not sick!"

His eyes crinkled. "Nope, never felt better. How about you?"

"I'm good." She hitched her thumb toward the bathroom. "But Cass doesn't feel so hot."

The crinkles at the corners of his eyes disappeared, replaced by deep furrows across his brow. "Do you think she was drugged?"

"I don't know what to think." Jen chewed her bottom lip, certain her sister wouldn't appreciate her sharing the gritty details of her affliction. "The roofie I was slipped has me seeing ghosts everywhere. But she refuses to go to sick bay."

"It could be a reaction to her change in diet," he said, not too convincingly. "I guess this means you two aren't up for the shore excursion."

"Jen, you still there?" Cass's voice trickled through the bathroom door.

"Yes. What can I do?"

"Go with Sam and Jake. Have a good time. Take my waterproof camera. Okay?"

Jen gave Sam a helpless look. "I don't think I should leave her."

His warm brown eyes held understanding. "She'd probably feel worse if you missed out on her account."

"You don't think I'm a bad sister to leave her alone when she's like this?"

"Not when she's telling you to go." He glanced at his watch. "And if we don't want to miss our ride to the river, we'd better get hopping."

"She did ask me to take lots of pictures." Jen grabbed the camera. "You'll be okay without me?" she called to Cass.

"Go."

Forty-five minutes later, Jennifer pressed a hand to her fluttering stomach at the sight of a big round rubber raft bobbing on the river, tied to shore by a single taut yellow rope.

The instant their guide handed her the orange life jacket and a waiver to sign, the butterflies had started. Oh, who was she kidding? These were honking big pterodactyls batting around her belly. Whatever possessed her to think she could do this? To think she could be back on the ship right now with her sister!

Sam's hand slipped around her waist. "You okay?"

"Sure," she squeaked. Swallowing, she tried again in a normal voice. "Uh, sure. Why do you ask?"

A dimple winked on his cheek, but the warmth in his eyes radiated genuine concern. "You're whiter than the glacier."

She made a face. "The glacier is blue."

"Yeah, you look a little blue, too. Breathe."

She gulped a breath.

"It's going to be fun, Jen. You'll see."

"Until the raft capsizes," she muttered.

The tour guide must've heard her, because he

loudly added something to the end of his safety spiel—the spiel she should've been paying more attention to. "Don't worry, we haven't had a raft capsize on us yet!"

"See," Sam said.

Jennifer hugged herself. "It's the 'yet' that worries me. You think I'm blue now. Do you know how cold that river is? It's glacial water, you know."

"You're not going in the water," Sam said firmly.

Uncomfortably aware of how childish her phobia must seem to him, she forced herself to stand tall.

His expression softened. "If you don't want to do this, we don't have to."

"No, I do." She certainly wasn't going to keep Jake and Sam from enjoying the excursion because she was chicken. And something told her she'd never be able to convince him to go on without her the way her sister had so easily convinced her. He wasn't like any other guy she'd ever met. At first he'd seemed a bit too interested in their art gallery, but maybe Cass was right—maybe he was just trying to show an interest in her life. He sure seemed concerned with her welfare.

She could do this. Conquer her fear. She shoved her hands into her parka's pockets and clasped Cass's camera.

Sam unbuckled his life jacket.

"What are you doing?" she blurted.

"I'm not going to urge you to do something you're terrified of." He peeled his jacket off his shoulders, slid it down his muscular arms, arms capable of plucking her from an icy fate…if need be. "We can hang out here and enjoy the view."

"I'm fine, really. Just a bit nervous. I want to do this." She held up the waterproof camera. "I have pictures to take."

Sam's lips spread into a proud grin—like the one she'd seen on his face when he'd watched his nephew jump into the pool without holding his nose. Well, no guarantees she wouldn't hold hers if they got dunked.

She shook away the thought. *Lord, please don't let the boat capsize or let me fall out. Please.*

A peace enveloped her. She suddenly felt silly about how much energy she'd wasted over worrying when she should've just been praying. Surrounded by the wondrous beauty of His creation she was a tad ashamed that she hadn't thought to pray sooner. Must've been the gargantuan effort she'd made to just plain ignore the fear knotting her gut from the moment they'd stepped on the minibus to bring them here.

Sam helped her into the boat then positioned himself behind her, with Jake in front.

With one hand holding the pocket camera poised, the other clamped around a handle on the raft, Jennifer held her breath as their guides pushed off.

The tour guide told them to all be quiet and just listen. The sound of silence was incredible. No traffic noises, no construction noises, no planes. Oh, cancel that. A seaplane glided over them toward the glacier. As it grew smaller, she heard other sounds. The babble of the river. The breeze whispering through the pines. The cry of a bird.

"Look!" A lady at the front of the raft pointed to the sky.

A bald eagle drifted lazily on the wind currents. Gasps rose from the group. Jennifer snapped a picture, wishing Cass could be here in person.

Sam leaned forward and squeezed her shoulder. "Enjoying yourself?"

She twisted around to smile at him. "This is amazing!"

They came to a bigger stretch of rapids and the group grew lively as the raft shot forward. Icy water splashed into their faces and they let out a collective scream.

Then a hush fell over them as a giant crack split the air. A huge chunk of blue ice broke off the glacier and splashed into the water. In fact, the water in front of the glacier was a minefield of tiny icebergs. One exquisitely blue berg split before their eyes with as loud a cracking noise as the piece that had broken away from the glacier moments earlier.

"That's incredible." Jen snapped a photo. "I wish I had video on this camera so I could capture the sound."

They lingered within view of the glacier for a long while.

"Look there." Sam pointed to a hunk of ice with something on it floating in the distance.

Jennifer zoomed in on it with her camera. "It's a

seal. Look." She handed Sam the camera. "It looks like it's sunbathing."

"You guys have lucked out with the weather today," the tour guide remarked. "June around here is usually cool, damp and foggy."

Instead they had sunshine and the thermometer had to be tickling sixty, even this close to a huge chunk of ice! She dipped her hand into the water and shivered at how cold it felt. No wonder the seal was sunbathing.

"The seal's not the only one basking in the sun." Sam pointed to another floating slab. "Look at those seagulls."

"Looks like they're having a block party," Jake quipped, snapping a picture.

Jennifer snapped a few of her own. *Thank you, Cass, for bullying me into this.* She inhaled deeply. She couldn't remember the last time she felt so content, at peace, awed by the beauty God created.

Too soon, the tour guide steered the raft ashore farther downriver.

Sam jumped out ahead of her and offered her his hand. The moment both her feet hit solid ground, he whooped. "You survived! Glad you came?"

She smiled so widely she felt her heart expand with it. "Absolutely. It was amazing Thank you. I'm sure I would've chickened out if not for you and Jake."

Jake climbed ashore behind her. "Our pleasure."

"The van will arrive in thirty minutes to return us to the ship," the guide announced. "Relax and enjoy the view until then. There's a couple of trails, but don't wander far. We do have bears around here."

After they shed their life jackets, Sam proposed they check out the trail leading into the woods. From the twinkle in his eyes, Jennifer suspected he was goading her—to see if she was as afraid of bears as she was of white-water rafting. But seeing passengers pull out their phones, she remembered that she still hadn't called that PI and this could be her last chance before leaving port. Cass was bound to be all over her for details about the tour as soon as she returned to the ship.

Except…she needed privacy and Sam seemed as determined as ever to stick to her side.

Spotting an outhouse, she motioned in its direction. "Um, if you'll excuse me a minute I, uh—" she stuffed her hands in her pocket "—need some privacy."

Sam chuckled.

Jennifer traipsed toward the outhouse. Yeah, she must've looked pretty silly getting flustered over needing to use the john, except that she didn't need to, and she hadn't wanted to lie and suddenly felt super guilty about the pretense when they'd been so sweet to her all afternoon. She tugged on the outhouse door.

"Someone's in here," a voice chimed.

Perfect. Jennifer peeked back around the outhouse. Sam and Jake were standing by the water talking with the tour guide. With the outhouse hiding their view of her, she edged into the trees, pulled her cell phone from her zippered pocket and removed it from the plastic bag she'd wrapped it in just in case. No signal. *Figures.*

She followed the trail to a small cliff near the shore, up a few hundred yards from where Sam and Jake stood. Two bars appeared on her cell phone screen. *Yes.* She found the PI's number she'd saved into the phone this time and hit dial.

A movement in her peripheral vision made her jump. What did the guide say about bears? Oh, no, why couldn't she remember?

Play dead for grizzlies. That's it. And run like you know what for black bears. Except…she was cornered between whatever kind of bear it was and the water!

Trying not to move a muscle, she scanned the ground for a good-sized branch. If she couldn't run, she could go out swinging. Maybe catch the thing on its snout.

A twig snapped behind her. Heavy breathing. No wait, that was her. She sucked in a breath, snatched up a nearby branch and swirled to face her foe.

A hairy, hulking guy rushed her, both arms straight out like twin battering rams.

She swung the wood, but he was quicker. He caught the branch midswing and jerked it from her grasp.

"Help!" she screamed, an instant before the wood slammed into her gut and sucked the air from her lungs.

Arms windmilling, she reeled backward. Her foot hit air.

Rocks, trees, sky spun past her. Then the slap of glacial water swallowed her whole.

SEVEN

Mark hasn't left ship, said the text message from the Juneau FBI agent Sam had contacted after learning Cass and Jennifer planned to split up this morning. Didn't mean Jen's sister hadn't gotten up to something illegal with the onboard art gallery or maybe a passenger. But more likely she really had been sick, not just trying to get her sister out of the way.

A scream, swallowed by a splash, gripped Sam's heart. His gaze snapped to the outhouse.

The door opened and a gangly teen stepped out.

"Jen!" Sam raced up the shoreline.

"There!" Someone standing on the bank above him pointed upriver.

Sam spotted Jen flailing in the icy water, the current pulling her toward them.

Jake grabbed a life ring, wrapped the rope around his hand and tossed it into her path. "Grab the ring!"

But Jen's head disappeared beneath the water, her blond hair swirling in the eddies.

Sam stripped off his jacket and shirt. "She's not going to make it."

"You can't go in after her." The tour guide and his assistant jumped in the raft and pushed off. "The water's too cold. You'll just be someone else we have to rescue."

Jake grabbed Sam's arm. "He's right. Your muscles will cramp and you'll be useless to her."

Sam jerked out of his hold. "I'm not going to stand by and let someone else die."

Jen's face broke through the water's surface, terror in her eyes.

"Hold on, Jen. We're coming." Sam ran along the shore as Jake hauled in the life ring.

She flailed her arms, gulping air.

The guys on the raft veered toward her. "Grab on," they shouted, but the current whisked her past them.

Sam grabbed the life ring from Jake. "Hang on to that rope," he shouted and dove into the river. His muscles seized instantly. Arm through the ring, he clawed to the surface with a roar, the fire in his blood overpowering the paralyzing pain. Where was she?

He twisted every which way. Water blurred his vision. He would not let her die the way he let— He swallowed the boulder-sized lump that caught in his throat and dug into the water.

"To your right," Jake shouted from shore.

With a powerful kick, Sam surged toward her. For a fleeting second, he caught strands of hair. But they slipped through his fingers. The life ring was slowing him down. He started to pull out his arm.

"Don't you dare let go," Jake ordered.

Sam kicked harder. She'd been under too long. "Jen!"

Her face broke the surface with a giant gasp. Her wild-eyed gaze slammed into his, clinging for dear life.

He plowed toward her, scarcely feeling his arms and legs.

"Sam," she breathed then dropped below the dark surface.

"No!" His leg scraped a rock. Kicking off it, he surged into her path and caught her around the waist. "I got you. Hang on."

She went limp in his arms.

As Jake hauled on the rope, Sam prayed for the strength to hold on. "Stay with me, Jen. You're going to be okay."

Her head lifted, eyes fluttering. With one arm hooked through the ring and one hooked around her waist, he didn't have a free hand to wipe the hair from her face. "Grab the ring, Jen. Hold on."

Her shivers vibrated through his own numb limbs. His eyes closed, his adrenaline rapidly draining. *So cold.* His arm clamped tighter around her waist. "I won't let you go." He tried to kick, but his legs had stopped cooperating. People were shouting at them, but their voices sounded far away.

All of a sudden Jen disappeared from his arms.

"No!" The shout ripped from his chest.

The stench of smoke filled his nostrils. Someone held him back. *No, not again. Not again, Lord.* His aunt's wails pounded his ears. He didn't know Jimmy was hiding in there. He didn't know. "Let me go, I've got to save—"

"It's okay. We got her."

Her? Not little Jimmy. Jen. Strong arms hooked under his and hauled him into the raft, free of the water's icy grip. He scrambled to see Jen.

She plunged into his arms. "You saved me." Her words slurred. She shivered violently—they both did. A scratchy blanket swallowed them, but just the sight of Jen alive, the sound of her voice, the feel of her arms slipping around his waist warmed him to the core.

He swept wet strands of hair from her face, his heart tumbling into her shimmering blue gaze. "I told you I'd keep you safe."

Her lips, as blue as her eyes from the cold, quivered into a smile.

He brushed a gentle kiss over those beautiful lips. They tasted like crisp spring days, fresh, *alive.* He wrapped her in his arms and pulled her closer. Somewhere in the back of his ice-numbed mind, a voice hissed out a warning, but he couldn't make sense of it.

Jake's voice penetrated Sam's hazy thoughts as someone hauled Jen from his arms. "Keep them horizontal." The men from the raft laid them on a blanket and covered them with jackets and hats. Someone started rubbing Jen's limbs. "Don't do that." Jake motioned the person back. "It'll only cause cold blood to flow back to her body core and cool it further." Jake placed two fingers at the pulse point on her throat and studied his watch.

Lying on his side next to her, still shivering despite the blankets and coats piled on him, Sam reached for her hand. Her eyes were closed, her breathing slow and shallow. "Is she ooo-kkkay?" he asked, his teeth chattering uncontrollably.

Jake dropped his hand from her pulse and lifted one eyelid. "She's moderately hypothermic. Her pulse is slow, pupils dilated."

"What?" she mumbled as Jake lifted the other eyelid.

"Shouldn't we get herrr out of thozzz wet clothes?" Jake pressed Sam's pulse point.

"Don't worry 'bout meee." Why did he sound like a drunk?

"You're hypothermic, too, you idiot. Who did you think you were, Superman? And invincible to the cold?" He dropped Sam's wrist. "Your pulse is normal. You're lucky."

Sam reached for Jen's hand, but she was gone. His eyes shot open. "Where's Jen?"

"Paramedics are loading her…out of the wet clothes before…body heat."

Sam's ears buzzed as he struggled to get to his feet, only catching half of what Jake said.

"Whoa, there." Jake pressed him to the ground. "Don't worry. They won't leave without you."

Next thing Sam knew he was levitated onto a

gurney. It bumped and rattled over the rough ground, making his head pound.

They let Jake ride in the ambulance with them. Confident his brother would watch out for Jen, Sam gave in to the exhaustion tugging at his eyes.

The barn rafters creaked as he raced for the last horse stall. He yanked his shirt over his mouth and nose against the smoke choking his lungs. Flames licked up the walls, seconds from torching the hayloft.

"It's too late. Get out of there," his father shouted from the barn door.

Sam threw open the stall and jumped out of the way as the horse charged for the door.

"Jimmy! Where's Jimmy?" his aunt screamed.

Jimmy's head popped up above the hay in the loft. "I'm up—" His eyes went round as Frisbees as he caught sight of the fire.

"Jimmy!" Sam sprinted toward the ladder.

His uncle grabbed him off the bottom rung and scrambled up after his son himself.

"No!" Sam screamed a second before the fire flashed over.

"Sam." Someone shook his shoulders. "Sam, wake up. It's just a dream."

Oh, how he wished that were true. He curled his arms against his chest and squeezed his eyes tighter.

The bed dipped beside him. Soft hands cupped his face. "Sam, you saved me. We're okay."

Recognizing Jen's voice, he clambered out of the memory, remembered instead catching hold of Jen. Sam closed his hands over hers and opened his eyes.

"You're—" He cleared the hoarseness from his throat. "You're okay?"

"Thanks to you." Her lips curved into the sweetest smile.

His heart shifted. He had a vague memory of tasting those lips and wondered if it had been a dream or real.

"Hey." Jake appeared in his line of vision, standing over his bed. "How do you feel?"

Jen pulled away and Sam pushed onto his elbows. "Out of shape."

"Yeah, Jen's a faster recoverer than you, apparently."

Sam glanced around what appeared to be an emergency room with multiple curtained-off beds. "What time is it?"

Jake glanced at his watch. "Five o'clock. Our tour guide offered to give us a lift in his van back to the ship. Mom sent dry clothes with him." Jake plopped a shirt and pair of jeans on Sam's chest. "I'll go ask the doctor if you both have the green light to leave."

Jen already wore a cozy pink sweater and dark slacks. Her hair had dried into soft curls around her rosy cheeks. Not a tint of blue anywhere. *Thank you, Lord.*

He snatched up his clothes and ducked into the bathroom.

"I really appreciate what you did for me," Jen said as he returned.

He found himself swimming in her beautiful blue eyes and brought her hand to his lips. Tomorrow he'd worry about getting too close to a suspect. Tonight he was just relieved she was okay. He sat on the edge of the bed to put on his shoes.

Jen pulled up a chair beside him. "Who's Jimmy?"

His heart clenched. "Jimmy?" The name came out choked.

Empathy brimmed in her eyes. "You were calling for him. I thought at first you were saying Jenny, but Jake said no. He wouldn't tell me who Jimmy was, said I should ask you."

Yeah, he would. Sam shot a glare at his brother, who'd just stepped inside the door. "He was our cousin. He died in a barn fire when he was about Tommy's age. It was after my first year at college."

"Oh, Sam." Jen squeezed his hand. "How horrible. I'm so sorry."

He expelled a breath and pushed to his feet. "It was a long time ago."

"Yes, it *was*," Jake pointedly agreed.

Sam pressed his lips against a retort. Staying away was easier than facing the empty seats at family re-unions.

"I guess Lucy was his mother?"

A cold shiver slinked over his body at the real name of the woman who'd almost cost him his job with the FBI. He shot Jake a worried look. What else had he muttered in his sleep?

Panic gripped Jen as their van pulled up along-side the ship. It was massive. Sixteen decks high. Three and a half football fields long. And chances were good her attacker was on it, waiting for another chance to strike.

She clutched the armrests. She could fly home. But was home any safer? For all she knew the knife in her car had been courtesy of the same guy. If only she knew what he wanted.

She squeezed her eyes shut. Wasn't it obvious?

He wanted her dead.

"You okay?" The concern in Sam's voice drew her from her black thoughts.

Her eyes sprang open. "Yes, I'm good." He'd promised to keep her safe, and he had. The last thing she wanted was to cause him more worry, or worse, cause him to blame himself for what happened as he obviously did in his cousin's death. She followed him out of the van and slipped her hand into his. He'd said little on the drive over, and she felt bad for rousing memories he'd clearly just as soon have left buried.

Or maybe he was worried she'd read more into his rescue than he wanted.

She revisited the moment his arm closed around her waist in the water, of his declaration, "I won't let you go."

Inhaling the crisp sea air, she lingered in the memory. She knew better than to think he'd meant forever, but his promise had given her hope when all seemed lost.

She touched her lips, remembering his tender kiss. It had lasted mere seconds, but she still felt its warmth.

He squeezed her hand as they started up the gangplank. "Your sister is going to kill me for letting you fall into the water."

Jen stopped. "I didn't fall." She'd forgotten that the doctor hadn't wanted to rouse him when the detective came to the emergency room to question her. "Sam, I was pushed."

Fear flared in his eyes, renewing her own panic. He spun toward Jake. "We need to notify the authorities. We've already lost—"

"They know." Jake urged them forward. "The detective has interviewed everyone on our tour, has other officers verifying the whereabouts of passengers who were off the ship at the time of the incident and should have the picture of every passenger who can't be accounted for, along with those on our tour, queued up for Jen to look through."

Sam blinked, clearly struggling to absorb all that he'd missed. "That's good." Sam's gaze skimmed the faces of those watching the pier from the decks above and he tugged her closer. "So you saw who pushed you?"

The trembling that had taken her hours to quell returned full force. "He was big. Had dark hair and a beard."

"Could it have been the same guy you saw in your cabin? The beard could've been fake."

"I don't know. It all happened so fast, and he was wearing sunglasses."

"Did you recognize him from the tour?"

She made a face. "I was too panicked about riding the rapids to pay attention to anyone else on the tour."

"It's okay." He curled his arm around her shoulders. "We'll find him."

As soon as they boarded the ship, a uniformed crew member escorted them to the security office. "The detective is waiting in here." The middle-aged woman with close-cropped brunette hair, and a ready smile, stood and stretched out a hand to Sam. "I'm Detective Reed. I'm handling the investigation." She motioned Jen to take the seat she'd vacated in front of the computer.

As Jen looked through the pictures that the detective had ready for her, Sam and Jake quizzed her on what she'd learned so far. Which amounted to nothing. None of the other passengers on their tour remembered the hulking, bearded guy in mirror sunglasses.

Jen fought the despair closing in on her. The faces on the screen all started to look the same and nothing like the guy who'd pushed her. She shook her head. "It's no use. The beard and glasses practically hid his entire face. Put him in a bulky parka and he could be any of these guys."

Sam squeezed her shoulder. "Take your time."

"Have you given any more thought to why someone would target you?" the detective asked.

Jennifer's breath caught in her throat. "No, I'm sorry."

"Miss Robbins," the detective implored. "This man deliberately pushed you into a glacial river. He clearly didn't expect you to live. We need to know *why* he targeted you."

"But I don't know why." Between the detective's questions and the video surveillance screens flickering around her, she felt as if she were drowning all over again.

"Do you have any enemies?" the detective pressed.

"No!" Jen dug her teeth into her bottom lip to keep it from quivering.

"Business rivals?"

"No. I assess grant applications for a charitable foundation. I told you this already."

Sam gently squeezed her shoulder again, grounding her. If he weren't here, they'd probably have to cart her off to a mental ward.

The detective turned a page in her notepad. "What about the family business? Any crooked associate who might threaten your safety to get what he wants from those who run the gallery?"

Jen's heart ricocheted off her ribs at how close to her fears the question hit. She forced herself to take deep breaths to slow her runaway pulse. She'd almost been killed. She needed to tell the detective about her suspicions of Uncle Reggie, but what about Cass? She was bound to get caught up in any investigation of Reg. Maybe be implicated in his crimes. Jen had to talk to her first.

Seeing Jen on the verge of falling apart under the detective's relentless questions, Sam wished he could have a "do over." He never should've talked her into going out today, let alone let her out of his sight. Never mind that he'd scanned every passenger's face when they boarded the bus and had made a point of talking to each one, listening for an Eastern European accent like the waiter who'd brought Jen the tainted drink. He would have had just as much opportunity to earn her trust and ply her for information if they'd stayed aboard, maybe more.

His cell phone rang. Checking the screen, he apologized to Jen and the detective. "I need to take this." Pressing his phone to his ear, he slipped out of the small security office. "What do you got?"

"You were right about the guy who bought the painting. His name is Sal Monticello and he's suspected of having mob connections."

The usual elation at learning his hunch had been right didn't come. Considering how forcefully Cass had dissuaded him from bidding, she had to be in on the deal. And for Jen's sake, he hadn't wanted her to be. Not that he was all that sure of Jen's innocence.

"Customs will have a welcoming committee waiting for him when he returns to Seattle," the FBI agent went on. "If he's smuggling stolen art, we'll find it."

The delight in his voice was unmistakable. Often art crime investigations resulted in recovering stolen pieces without ever making an arrest. The more valuable the piece, the more likely the thief would find it impossible to unload without getting caught and in the end would let it go for a fraction of its value just to get it off his or her hands.

Sam filled the agent in on what happened to Jen. "Find out everything you can on Monticello. Figure out what kind of hold he has on the Robbins Gallery.

Could be he was threatening Jen to coerce her sister into cooperating. If that painting he bought at auction didn't deliver what he'd expected, that'd explain the finality of today's attack."

Jake exited the security office, giving Sam a glimpse of Jen's harrowed expression. His chest tightened. "I've got to go." Clicking off his phone, he asked his brother, "What's going on in there?"

"More of the same. I'm going up to check on Tommy and to let Mom and Dad know we're safely aboard."

Sam pulled him aside, away from the crew members staffing the concierge counter, and lowered his voice. "Back at the hospital, what did I say about Lucy?"

Jake chuckled. "Afraid you blew your cover?"

"I—"

Jake cut him off with a lift of his hand. "Save the denials. There is something you need to know. I didn't get the chance to tell you before because I didn't want to worry Jen."

"What?"

"When Mom knocked on Cass's door to get dry clothes for Jen, Cass didn't answer."

Sam tensed at the thought of what she could've been up to all day. He'd had a man on her—at least as close as he could get one. Obviously not close enough.

"Mom convinced the steward to check the room, afraid Cass had taken a turn for the worse. Cass wasn't there. Mom checked the clinic and around the ship but never found her. She ended up buying the outfit for Jen at the boutique because the steward couldn't allow her to take anything from the room."

"See if you can locate her, will you?" Sam said. "Then call down and let me know right away."

"Will do."

Sam scrubbed a hand over his face. *What a mess.* Clearly Cass's *illness* had been a ploy to get Jen to go on the excursion alone. Best-case scenario—she had an art deal scheduled that he'd missed scoping out. Worst-case scenario...

She'd hired that guy to attack Jen.

Sam's stomach revolted at the thought. But Cass had more motive than anyone. The inheritance that came into their full control in mere days would be all hers. Or maybe Jen's intimation yesterday that she wanted to sell the gallery roused Cass's fears that Jen would screw up their lucrative sideline in art fraud.

His stomach wrenched into knots. How could he protect Jen from her own sister?

Catching herself twisting her hands in her lap, Jen splayed her fingers over her thighs and took another deep breath. "I already told you that I wouldn't know. I don't get involved with the gallery's business."

"I'm trying to help you, Miss Robbins," Detective Reed reiterated.

"I know. I'm sorry."

Sam returned to the room, and the detective's gaze lifted to his for a moment.

Reed flipped to a clean page in her notebook. "Who knew you'd be on this particular excursion today?"

Jennifer let out a frustrated sigh. There was obviously no escaping the woman's questions. And maybe she was in serious denial to want to.

"Miss Robbins?"

Jennifer flung up her arms in frustration. "I don't know. Whichever crew members have access to that information, Sam here, his brother and parents. Nobody who'd want to kill me!"

"Did a travel agent handle the booking?"

"I don't know. The cruise was a gift from our uncle. My sis—ter…booked the excursions." Jen's gaze snapped to Sam's. *It couldn't be Cass.*

The office door jerked open and Cassie stumbled in, followed by Jake.

Jennifer sprang to her feet.

"Jen, are you okay?" Cassie flung her arms around her. Her breath stank of beer. She wore a skintight tank and leather miniskirt that she'd promised Jennifer she'd leave at home in favor of more modest choices.

Jen disentangled herself from her sister's arms. "What have you been doing?"

"Oh, Jen, I'm sorry I wasn't here for you. Jake told me what happened," she slurred. "I feel terrible."

Sam looked as if he could spit nails. "Where'd you find her?"

"The bar," Jake muttered. "She had quite an entourage buying her drinks." Jake reported, amazingly without a hint of the disgust he must feel.

"Never mind that." Cass stroked Jen's hair, looking genuinely worried. "Are you okay?"

Jen's stomach roiled at the reek of beer. She pushed her away. "I thought you were sick, Cass. That's why you didn't come on the excursion. Remember? What were you doing at the bar?"

"I started feeling better and I got bored." She shrugged. "I lost track of time or I woulda been in the room when you got back."

"Five hours ago?" Sam seethed, his tone colder than the Mendenhall River. "'Cause that's when you *should have* expected her."

Jennifer's heart rate took off at a gallop. Sam's words—*sometimes we don't know people as well as we think we do*—streaked through her mind. He suspected Cass!

But Cass couldn't be behind the attacks. *She wouldn't.* Sure, she planned the excursions, and then…insisted Jen go on her own because she was too sick.

Jennifer shook her head. No, her sister wouldn't plot to kill her.

Except… What if Uncle Reggie had so corrupted her he'd convinced her that Jen needed to die?

No! The idea was ridiculous. Cass could never be party to killing her only flesh and blood.

"I'm sorry, Jen," Cass purred. "You know how I lose track of time when I'm occupied. I knew you'd be safe with Sa-a-am." She gave Sam's name two extra syllables and twirled his shirt collar with her finger.

Sam caught Cass's finger and gave her a hard

stare. "Your sister could have died. Do you understand that?"

"I—" Cass whimpered, her expression crumbling.

Jake grabbed her by the waist and pulled her away from his brother. "Take it easy, Sam. It's not as if Cass pushed her."

Great, now her problems were putting Sam and his brother at odds. Although she had to admit his indignation felt really sweet.

Sam's eyes shot daggers at his brother. Clearly he suspected that Cass had been drinking to drown a guilty conscience, but unfortunately, Cass in this condition was nothing new.

"Are we done, Detective?" Jennifer asked quietly, eager to get away before the detective got the same idea.

The woman glanced at her watch. "Once this ship sails, so does any further chance of my helping you."

Jen cringed. "I understand."

"Okay." Reed closed her notebook and shot a glance Cass's way before adding, "Watch your back."

Sam lagged behind to have a word with the detective.

Cass looped her arm through Jennifer's. "What do you say we go to the all-you-can-eat buffet? I'm starved."

"It's almost nine o'clock, Cass." And despite her long rest in the hospital, she was bone tired from answering the detective's questions. A sensation of being watched made her skin tingle. She glanced around the lobby, up the open staircases to the other levels overlooking it.

"So…" Cass carried on. "The buffet's open all night."

"Count me out. I promised Tommy I'd take him to watch the movie under the stars," Jake glanced at his watch. "And it starts in fifteen minutes. I'll see you later."

Jennifer waved after him. "Thanks for finding my sister for me, Jake."

He threw a grin her direction. "Anytime."

Sam rejoined them and agreed to dinner more readily than she'd expected after his blowup at Cass.

"I kind of thought you'd rather we order room service and stay out of sight until the police catch whoever pushed me."

Sam's gaze slanted momentarily in Cass's direction as he guided them to the elevator. "I'm not ready to let you out of *my* sight."

He made it sound romantic, but the protective edge to his voice said he was dead serious. She cringed at her word choice.

Cass wouldn't look at him. No doubt she was still smarting from his scolding. Seeing her sister's condition tonight only reinforced Jen's fears of what would become of Cass if she didn't coax her out of the art gallery business. Unfortunately, her condition also proved how tainted she'd already become.

Please, Lord, don't let her be too tainted to listen to reason.

Stepping into the spacious buffet room at the bow

of the ship, Sam handed Jen a plate. She meandered past the salad bar without really seeing the food. After she passed the appetizers, too, her plate empty save for a bread stick, Sam elbowed her. "If we're going to switch plates tonight I hope you're going to put a lot more than that on yours."

She smiled. "I think I'll feel safe eating from my own plate tonight." Her gaze skittered around the near-empty dining area. Who was she kidding? She wasn't going to feel safe any time soon.

They settled at a table with a view of the harbor. In another hour they'd be able to watch the ship slip back out to sea, thanks to the infamous Alaskan midnight sun. And for how jittery her insides felt, Jen was pretty sure she'd still be wide awake.

The sight of someone using a cell phone on the outside deck reminded her that she'd never gotten hold of the PI. She reached into her pocket only to shake her head at her silliness. How could she have forgotten that she wasn't even wearing the same clothes?

"What's wrong?" Sam asked.

"I just realized that I must have lost my cell phone when I fell in the river."

He reached into his pocket. "You're welcome to use mine."

"No, that's okay." She waved off his offer. "I lost the number with it." And she didn't feel like asking the art gallery curator a third time for the stupid thing. Maybe God was trying to tell her something... like don't call the PI.

"What's the name?" He pulled up the internet. "I can look it up."

"It's fine. It can wait until I get back to Seattle." She hoped.

"What excursion is your family taking tomorrow?" Cass asked, as if a giant monkey wrench hadn't just been tossed into their plans.

Sam stopped sawing the beef slab he'd been working on and met Jen's gaze. "Whichever one you're on…if you feel up to it."

"Of course she'll feel up to it," Cass gushed. "I can't miss another tour!"

After the way he'd seen Cass tonight, Jennifer was sure the last place Jake would want to be tomorrow was on a tour with her sister. He'd just been being nice with that "anytime" quip. Not to mention Jen needed some alone time with Cass if she was going to have any chance of convincing her to sell.

"Um." Jennifer shuffled the food around on her plate before finally spearing a pickle. "I thought we had an appointment in Skagway to pick something up for Uncle Reggie."

Cass sloughed off her concern with a flip of her hand. "We'll have plenty of time. The ship won't leave port until eight."

"That means we have to be back on by seven."

"It won't be a problem. The train gets back into Skagway by midafternoon. We're booked on the White Pass Summit Excursion. It's a scenic railway that takes us all the way to the summit."

Jen's insides tumbled. *Summit?* "I don't think I'll feel up—"

"We have to go, Jen. It'll be fun. Take your mind off what happened."

What happened. *What happened?* Could Cass really be so oblivious to how serious this was? Did she think what happened today was nothing worse than when their raft capsized in high school?

She'd clearly missed the fact the river water was *glacial and she had been pushed in by an attacker.* "You know, Cass, even you, with all your high school swimming medals, wouldn't have been able to swim long in that frigid water today."

Cass frowned. "How wide a river are we talking?"

"What does it matter?" Jen blurted then immediately lowered her voice. "You don't seem to get that someone wants me dead."

EIGHT

Unable to sleep for worrying about leaving Jen alone with her sister, Sam slipped out onto the balcony. The foghorn blared a long, lonely sound. It was 5 a.m., and it had already been light for hours, but that didn't stop the damp, chilly air from seeping through his clothes.

He zipped up the windbreaker he'd thrown on and squinted in the direction Skagway should be.

The mist rolling over the water obscured the view of land, kind of how he felt about this case—if he didn't get his bearings soon, he might just run aground. The fact that almost getting killed hadn't been enough to convince Jen to divulge her secrets made it look as though she was as neck deep in the art fraud as her sister and guardian.

His mind flipped back to last night. Who had Jen wanted to call?

Clearly someone she hadn't wanted him, or maybe her sister, to know about. Because his background check had offered no indication of a significant other in her life, he suspected John Watson, the PI, whose number she'd gotten from the gallery curator. He wanted to believe she had the PI's number because she was as anxious to get to the truth as he was.

But he was running out of time. If she and her sister walked out of the gallery this afternoon with the stolen painting, the local feds would arrest them both before they had enough information to tie the sale to Michaels.

He thumbed his boss's number on his cell phone and sank onto the lounge chair, listening to the water lap against the ship's hull and the low hum of the engines. "Learn anything more on the mob connection?" he asked when his boss came on the line. If the smuggling was connected to organized crime and Jen had stuck her nose where it didn't belong, they could be looking at a hit man who came to Juneau to do the job the waiter messed up.

"Our informant said he hadn't heard about any double cross that would compel the family to take revenge on your suspect."

Sam cringed at the reference to Jen as a suspect. She might be keeping secrets, but she didn't throw *herself* into the river.

On the other side of the balcony divider, a scuffle erupted.

"Gotta go," he hissed into the phone then crammed it into his pocket.

"No, no. Stay away."

Fire shot through his veins at Jen's muffled plea. He scaled the balcony rail and started to swing around the partition. At the sight of her wrestling a blanket in her lounge chair, he stopped short. "Jen," he said softly, crouched on the rail at the partition separating their balconies.

She flailed her arms and whipped from side to side, her moans rising in panic.

He jumped onto her balcony and hunkered down at her side. "Jen," he whispered. "It's just a dream."

Perspiration beaded her forehead as she continued to flail about.

He clasped her arms through the blanket. "Jen," he said more firmly. "You're okay. Wake up." What was she doing sleeping out here anyway?

He glanced through the balcony door at her darkened room and uneasiness rippled through his chest. Was she afraid to sleep in the same room as her sister? More afraid of her sister than her balcony-climbing prowler?

Her eyes squeezed tighter, her face contorted in anguish.

He smoothed the hair from her face. "Jen, honey, you need to wake up." His heart double-Dutched at the endearment. He jerked his hand back to his side. What was he doing?

Her eyes flew open. "Sam?" Her gaze jumped from him to the partition to the balcony door to the wall of fog beyond the rail and back to him. "What are you doing here?"

"You cried out. I thought you were in trouble."

"I must've been dreaming." She tugged her blankets to her chin.

He stroked the lines they'd made on her cheek. "Why are you sleeping out here?"

"I couldn't sleep. Every time I closed my eyes I saw his face, saw him lunging toward me." She shivered.

Against his better judgment, Sam folded her in his arms. He couldn't help himself. She looked utterly stricken. He wanted to say "It's okay. You're safe now." But he didn't know that. In fact, he doubted it with every ounce of his being. This was no act to dupe him into sympathizing with her. She trembled against his chest and he tightened his hold.

"Why did he do it?" she mumbled. "Why?"

This was his chance to get the information he needed, to breach her defenses while her guard was down. Later he could hate himself for taking advantage of her vulnerability.

"Why do *you* think, Jen?" He loosened his embrace but continued to hold her in his arms. Her vanilla scent replaced the salty mist filling his nostrils. Her warmth… He jerked his thoughts back to his question.

She shook her head against his chest. "I don't know."

They'd already been down this road. He needed to coax her to face the suspicions she was too afraid to voice. "What's changed in your life recently?"

He clasped her arms and set her back from him, enough to look into her eyes. Her pure blue eyes, the color made all the more vivid thanks to the moisture pooling there.

"Nothing." She answered without pausing to think, so he waited. He could see in her eyes the thoughts whirring through her mind.

She ducked her head. "Nothing. Same job. Same apartment. Same church. Same friends."

"You're turning twenty-five. You're telling me you haven't thought about making a change or two in your life?"

A muscle in her cheek ticked. "I'm not desperate to find a husband, if that's what you mean."

He chuckled. "Not what I meant." He waited, not about to reveal that he knew the significance of her twenty-fifth birthday.

She squirmed under his steady gaze. The ship's engines wound down, signaling their arrival at the dock.

She drew a deep breath and let it out slowly. "On our twenty-fifth birthday, Cass and I gain control over our parents' estate."

Sam whistled as if this were news to him, even though she'd alluded to as much at the art auction. "That's a biggie."

"Yeah. I want to sell the gallery, something our guardian has always refused to consider. Now that the choice will be ours, I'd hoped to convince Cass to sell, too."

Because of the gallery's illegal dealings? Did she think she could escape charges by getting out?

"You think I'm terrible, don't you?"

He jerked back, unnerved that she seemed to have read his thoughts. "No, why would you say that?"

"Because it was our parents' baby." Guilt colored her voice.

He knew all about not living up to family expectations. "You need to do what's right for you. Be where God wants you to be." His chest tightened at that last part. He'd meant it to prick her conscience, not his own.

"You're right." She looked at him with a seemingly new appreciation. "Except…I'm not sure where that is, but my heart has never been in Seattle. We used to live in a small rural community. Mom would sell commissioned pieces and teach private art classes. Dad managed a store. Life was simple. People were real."

"What happened?"

"Mom got discovered and our life changed overnight." Melancholy edged her words. "We moved to the city, started the gallery and the new life consumed them. We used to do things together, go to church, visit with friends afterward. Real friends."

Inside the cabin, Cass stirred. He didn't have much time. But Jen's motive was becoming clearer than ever. "When did you tell Cass you wanted to sell?" If the attacks started soon after…

"I haven't yet."

Okay, not what he expected to hear. "Who have you told?"

"I made discreet inquiries, hoping to quietly find a buyer before I talked to Cassie."

"And have you found a buyer?"

"Yes, last week. I'd planned to tell Cass at the restaurant—that night my car was vandalized—but she was going on about the cruise Reggie had just surprised us with and I never got the chance."

Sam slanted a glance through her balcony doors

and back to her. "Are you sure Cass and your uncle hadn't already heard?"

Fear flickered in Jen's eyes. She curled her blanket to her chest, drawing up her knees.

Sam rubbed her upper arms. "Think about it. The attacks started after you found a buyer."

"I know what you're thinking. But you're wrong. We may have our differences, but Cass would never hurt me." Jen's voice was assured, but uncertainty hovered in her eyes.

"And your guardian?"

She swallowed. "He'd be upset, naturally. He's been the gallery's curator for fifteen years. But he wouldn't gain anything by hurting me."

"Except stopping the sale."

Jen's brow furrowed, but she didn't respond.

Sam tried a different tack. "What about Cass's boyfriend?"

"She doesn't have a particular one."

"Is there one she sees more than the others?" When Jen didn't answer, he added, "One who might be more interested in her money than in her?"

Jen snorted. "The story of our lives."

She said it with disgust, but Sam didn't miss the hurt vibrating beneath her words. He steeled himself against a rush of anger toward the jerk who'd put it there. If he wasn't careful, he'd soon be the next such jerk in her life. Who was he kidding? He already was.

He put a lid on that train of thought and focused on the questions. "How about one who thought she'd turn to him for comfort if she lost you?" Someone like a trusted guardian?

Jen's gasp nearly undid him. Her face paled.

Now they were getting somewhere. "You have someone in mind?"

"Our guardian's son, Blake. He's four years older than us. Cass has had a crush on him since the day Uncle Reggie took us into his home. Blake was already off at college, but he'd come home weekends and holidays."

"They dated?"

"Not really. Blake is as much a playboy as Cass is a flirt. But she could always count on him to escort her to the important events."

Sam made a mental note to have the Seattle office run a background check. Her guardian's son had scarcely been a blip on their radar. Clearly he warranted a second look.

Jen shook her head. "But what would he gain from hurting me?"

The disbelief in her voice didn't jibe with the way her face had paled only moments ago. Had she revealed more than she'd intended?

"It's what your sister gains. Don't you think?"

The balcony door jerked open. Cass stepped into the doorway, tugged her robe closed more tightly. Her eyes were bloodshot and wan looking without her usual gobs of mascara and eye shadow. "What's going on?"

"We were watching the sunrise," Sam said without thinking.

"Really?" Her gaze bypassed his shoulder to the thick wall of fog beyond the balcony rail. "Then I'll take first dibs on the shower. Don't wait too long for the sun to show up, Jen. We need to get to breakfast by eight if we don't want to miss our tour." She flounced back inside and slid shut the door.

Sam sat on the edge of Jen's lounge chair. "As a precaution, I switched our reservations from the railway to the bus tour. It'd be best if you don't mention the switch to Cass until absolutely necessary."

Jen opened her mouth as if she might defend her, but closing it again, she looked out over the balcony rail and frowned. "Something tells me we're not going to see much of anything today."

On the contrary, he was praying everything would become crystal clear. He squeezed her hands, hoping to draw her thoughts back to the conversation Cass had interrupted.

She met his questioning gaze and shook her head. "Blake is rich enough in his own right. He doesn't need my sister's money, let alone my share." Her voice quavered as if she wanted to believe it more than she did.

"In my experience, the richer the man, the more he wants."

Jen closed her eyes and a sigh seeped from her chest. "Can we not talk about this today? I want to at least *try* to enjoy the trip."

He released her hands. They weren't done talking about this. Not by a long shot. If his guess was right, this afternoon she and Cass were scheduled to pick up the stolen painting. Before then, he needed to figure out if either of them knew what they would really be transporting for their "uncle" Reggie. If they came clean before the FBI agents waiting in Skagway nabbed them, maybe he could offer a deal in exchange for helping nail Michaels.

He scrubbed his palm over his morning whiskers. He'd like to believe Jen was nothing but an innocent victim here, a victim of other people's greed. But her sudden interest in the FBI's National Database of Stolen Art had to have been sparked by something. And an honest, law-abiding citizen would have reported that something on the spot.

He straightened, distancing himself from the effect of her vulnerability on his heart. "Knock on our cabin door when you're ready to head up for breakfast. We'll join you." He clenched the balcony rail to swing back around to *his* side of the partition—where he should have stayed in the first place.

Oohs and ahhs rose from the passengers as their motor coach escaped the fog blanketing the lower miles of the Klondike Highway. The majestic vistas filled Jen's heart with praise. "Almost makes me want to burst out in song."

Seated next to the window, Cass laughed as she snapped photographs. "I can just see you like Julie Andrews in *The Sound of Music*."

Sam, who sat across the aisle from them, leaned her way for a better view because his side of the motor coach currently faced a cliff face. *"For the Beauty of the Earth,"* he said quietly, naming the exact hymn that had been humming through her mind.

They shared a smile. And in that moment, the other passengers aboard—Sam's brother and nephew sitting in front of him, his parents sitting in front of her and Cass—seemed to fade and it was just her and Sam, like they'd been on the balcony this morning.

When she'd dragged her pillow and blanket out to the lounge chair in the wee hours of the morning in a vain attempt to escape the nightmares, she'd felt so alone. The clouds had obscured the stars so that not even God seemed near. But maybe Sam had been God's answer to her prayers. When he'd jostled her from her nightmares and folded her in his comforting embrace, she'd never felt safer.

Surprisingly, that didn't scare her like it should. Maybe because she knew Sam would be flying back to his life in Boston after the cruise and couldn't have any ulterior motives for spending time with her.

At the sight of snow-tipped peaks, the bus driver narrating the drive with tales of the Gold Rush mentioned sled dogs. Tommy scrambled out of his seat beside Jake and, plopping his bottom onto Sam's lap, tugged on Jen's sleeve.

"I sled-ed-ed," he declared. "The husky pulled us across the glacier."

"Wow! That must have been super fun."

He nodded broadly. "Uh-huh, and I got to hold the puppies. They licked my face all over." He patted his fingers up and down his face in demonstration.

"Oh, what a treat! I love puppies."

"Me, too." He hopped off his uncle's lap and scurried back to his father. "Can we get a puppy, Dad? I'll take real good care of it."

"Famous last words," Sam murmured. Jen and Sam exchanged a mirthful look, one that felt as if they'd known each other for years instead of mere days, and a corner of her heart was sad that he lived on the East Coast.

Sam's mother scooped Tommy into her lap. "Maybe Grandpa and I should get a pup and you could come over and play with it anytime you want."

"Really?" Tommy's voice filled with greater wonder than the adults had expressed over the sights outside the window.

"Sure thing, Champ," his grandpa said. "About time we got ourselves a new dog."

Jennifer soaked in the warmth of this wonderful family. "Your parents are great," she whispered to Sam, and she hoped the catch in her voice didn't give away her longing for what she'd lost.

A strange look flickered in his eyes. Almost like guilt, except... No, she must've imagined it because his gaze warmed as it shifted to his parents and then his brother and nephew. "Yeah, I'm pretty blessed."

They traveled in companionable silence, listening to the driver recount tales of the men who'd trudged to the three-thousand-foot summit of White Pass and the incredible amount of provisions they'd had to prove they'd brought to sustain themselves before the Canadian Mounted Police would let them cross into Yukon territory. If she'd spent more time considering what she'd need to convince Cassie to sell the gallery, maybe she'd have been better prepared for this trip, too.

She'd hoped sitting beside each other in the relatively private seats of the motor coach would provide an opportunity to steer their conversation to this afternoon's appointment at the Skagway gallery and to her desire to get out of the family business. In fact, the situation had seemed ideal. Cassie wouldn't make a scene in front of a bus full of people. But Sam's proximity made Jennifer hesitate.

He was too inquisitive. If he caught wind of the illegal dealings she suspected Reggie of, he'd insist on telling the detective who investigated the attack. By the time they got back to Seattle the press would have gone rabid on the gallery, and she'd lose her buyer for sure.

The bus stopped at the United States–Canada border and a customs agent boarded the bus and checked each passenger's passport. He didn't check their bags or ask if they had anything to declare, which got her thinking how easy it would be to smuggle something across the border, which got her thinking about the stolen painting she'd spotted in their gallery's storage room. If she, who was rarely there, had noticed it—never mind that she'd been looking—could Cass really be oblivious to Uncle Reggie's criminal activities?

"Are you okay?" Sam jostled her arm—her still raised and trembling arm—holding up her passport for the border guard's perusal even though he'd already passed.

She hurriedly stuffed the passport in her jacket pocket. "Just daydreaming, I guess."

His gaze darkened with sympathy as if he thought she meant nightmare-type daydreams. It was probably better that way.

"Look." Cass pointed to the train that had also ground to a stop at the border on the other side of the highway. "That's the tour we would've been on."

"This is just as good, Cass. I'm glad Sam was able to arrange the last-minute switch. Aren't you?" Jen's pulse raced at the reason behind the switch. "I mean, I'd just as soon not be where I'm expected."

Cass rubbed at an invisible spot on her pant leg. "I'm sorry."

Jennifer poked her with her elbow. "I don't blame you. It's not like any of it was your fault, right?"

Cass didn't answer, just gazed out the window at the train.

Jennifer's heart stumbled over a beat or two. "Cass?"

"I don't know, Jen. I can't imagine why anyone would want to hurt *you*." She buttoned her too-open blouse a button higher. "You're the good sister."

It wasn't the first time Cass had called her that, but usually her tone wasn't flattering.

As what she'd said sank in, Jennifer's heartbeat filled her throat. "You *can* imagine someone wanting to hurt *you*?" They were twins. And although they didn't dress similarly or share the same taste in hairstyles and makeup, they could easily be confused by someone who didn't know them both.

Cass shrugged.

"Cass, if you know who was behind yesterday's attack, we need to tell the detective." Jennifer sensed Sam leaning their way again, his concern no doubt raised by the mention of the attack, and Jen suddenly remembered why they might not want to involve the detective.

"I don't know." Cass fiddled with her camera, scrolled through the images she'd captured. A half dozen of the train. "It's just with all the parties I go to and stuff, I'm the one who tends to attract the weirdos."

Did Cass really think that, or was she attempting to cast suspicion *off* herself? Jen shook Sam's suspicions from her head. Her sister occasionally called her dislike of attending gallery functions a holier-than-thou attitude, but Cass couldn't really despise her. Could she?

Twenty minutes later as Jen stood beside Cassie on the Yukon Suspension Bridge with nothing but a thin rope mesh between her and the roaring rapids fifty-seven feet below, Jen prayed she was right about her sister. Cass was, after all, the *one* person who knew she was *here*.

Sam's mom herded her sons and grandson close to her and Cass. "Let me get your picture."

Jen turned to face Mrs. Steele, but without the handrail to hold, she felt her stomach plummet to her toes.

Mrs. Steele backed up a few feet, studying the camera's screen. "Squeeze closer."

Sam's arm slipped around Jen's waist and her stomach somersaulted for a whole different reason.

"You're shaking." His touch on her back firmed reassuringly. "Afraid of heights?"

"Not heights. Just falling." The thunder of the rapids roused terrifying images of yesterday's plunge. She stiffened her spine. She would not let that creep— or her fears—ruin her vacation.

Sam urged her forward the instant his mom had her photograph. "Let's admire the view from the platform."

Sam's family surrounded them the entire time they were off the bus. It crossed Jennifer's mind that perhaps Sam had asked them to—safety in crowds and all that. Even though she should probably feel badly about intruding on their family time, especially on such a special trip, she couldn't bring herself to break away. But she'd have to soon if she wanted to talk to Cass about selling before their appointment this afternoon.

She had a bad feeling about what Uncle Reggie might be expecting them to bring back to Seattle. If they were caught transporting a stolen painting she doubted the police would believe that they didn't know it. And they'd be right...sort of. Did that make her a criminal, too?

No, if she was right about Uncle Reggie setting them up, she'd refuse to take the package, put the ultimatum to Cass then and there—sell the gallery, or face the consequences of working with a criminal.

Oh, Lord, I just want to sell the gallery and wash my hands of the whole thing. You can deal with Uncle Reggie however you see fit. Please let me convince Cass to get out before it's too late. I couldn't bear to lose her, too.

In no time they were back on the bus for the return trip. But they'd have one more stop—a salmon bake at the re-creation of a tent city, circa 1898.

As they pulled into the parking lot thirty minutes later, she wasn't sure what made her more edgy: the line of motor coaches and milling people, the dark forest where anyone could be hiding or the costumed actors portraying nineteenth-century crooks.

What if her attacker had learned about their excursion switch and waited for her here?

As if he'd read her mind, Sam pulled her hand through the crook of his arm. "I'll protect you from these smarmy blokes, milady."

Jake likewise escorted Cass, and they trounced off as one happy throng toward the grilling salmon. The aroma of the spruce kindling filled her senses and Jennifer soon lost herself in the spirit of the place, delighting in an old woman's violin playing and the good-natured squabble of a couple degenerate miners over a young wench rescued by a more reputable-looking young man.

"Will you join us for a tour of the Red Onion Saloon once we get back to Skagway?" Sam's dad asked, slipping his last bite of salmon to the massive malamute making puppy dog eyes at him.

"I'm afraid we can't. Cass and I have some business to attend to at one of the galleries in town."

"I can go on my own," Cass chimed in, "if you really want to check out the Red Onion."

"Are you kidding me? You were adamant about us going together." The thought niggled that that had been before the attack in Juneau, an attack that should've prevented her from joining Cass. She shut down the ridiculous notion. If she'd died, Cass would *not* have been making any trips to the Skagway gallery, alone or otherwise.

"It's not a big deal," Cass said.

"Yes, it is." She wasn't about to let Cass dig herself in deeper trouble by transporting one of Uncle Reggie's stolen paintings. "Uncle Reggie asked us both to go. We'll both go." She refrained from saying she wasn't about to let Cass go traipsing around Skagway alone.

But Sam must've read her thoughts. "I'd be happy to escort you. If you finish your errand early enough, we can meet up with my parents to stroll back to the ship together."

"No!" Heat flamed Jennifer's cheeks at how abruptly she'd responded. "I mean, we've intruded long enough on your family time."

"Nonsense." Sam's dad waved off the suggestion. "We've enjoyed every minute of your company."

"That's so sweet of you to say. It's been wonderful spending time with you, too, but there's no need for

Sam to miss your tour on our account." Jennifer excused herself to pick a dessert from the serving table, hoping Sam would follow if he intended to argue further. It was hard enough to resist one Steele without taking on the whole family. And the truth was, she was terrified at the prospect of walking Skagway's streets with only Cass at her side. But she couldn't let Sam in on their horrible secret and risk his going to the police.

His arm grazed hers as they reached for adjoining pie slices. "You can't possibly think I'd let you walk around Skagway alone after what happened yesterday."

The delicious shiver that had prickled her skin at his touch fizzled at his harsh tone.

"You have been wonderful to watch out for us, and I really appreciate it, but despite what your dad said, this is their fortieth wedding anniversary and I'm sure they'd like to enjoy some time with you to themselves."

"They adore you." He almost seemed to wince at the observation.

Did his parents' invitation bother him? No. If it had, he would've pounced on the out she'd given him. Maybe he was embarrassed by his mother's less-than-subtle matchmaking tactics. Her heart dropped a little at the possibility. Not that anything would come of the woman's efforts. It figures the first guy she'd met that *genuinely* seemed to want to spend time with her for herself, not her connections, lived on the other side of the country.

"And I adore your parents. But you need some time with just them." He started to protest, but she lifted her hand to silence him. "And I need some alone time with my sister. Okay?"

"It's not safe. You can be alone with her on the ship."

Jennifer should've known his mile-wide protective streak would present a problem. Never mind the happy whirl his caring spun her heart into.

NINE

Sam stood at the edge of the re-created tent city, watching Cass pose for a picture behind the scale at the assayer's office, and forced his fist to unclench. He didn't like it, but he'd relented to Jennifer's insistence and agreed to go to the Red Onion with his parents rather than escort her to the art gallery. Not that he intended to do any such thing. He didn't plan on letting the women out of his sight.

"Welcome to my world," his brother said, jabbing his shoulder.

"What are you talking about?" Sam kept his gaze fixed on Jen now mugging for the camera, hating the doubts that her exaggerated gloating over her pile of gold dust on the scale escalated.

Jake chuckled. "Rejection."

Sam didn't dignify his brother's goading with a response. Jennifer's rejection was the least of his problems. If she and her sister picked up the stolen painting as he expected, his men would move in and arrest her. He wouldn't be involved in the takedown, of course—he couldn't afford to jeopardize his undercover persona in the art world. But that wouldn't stop his family from concluding he was behind the arrests. For how fond they'd grown of the pair, or at least of Jen, they'd probably side with them, too, and disown *him*.

But even that likelihood didn't bother him as much as his disappointment in Jen. Apparently he hadn't been paying attention to the ticker tape message pinging in the back of his mind for the past three days, reminding him she was a suspect.

Jake elbowed his brother's ribs. "Hey, it's not the end of the world. She just wants to spend the afternoon with her sister. Probably in some misguided female way, she's trying to prove to you that she's not clingy or needy."

Sam switched his attention to a tourist outside the newspaperman's tent who seemed a little too interested in Jen's photo shoot. "You're an expert in women now?"

"Not all of them, but the female firefighters on my crew would sooner die than let one of the guys think they couldn't take care of themselves."

The effect of Jake's word choice—*die*—must've shown on his face because his brother immediately backpedaled. "Not literally. You know what I mean. A good firefighter always knows they can count on their partner."

Unfortunately, Jen wasn't a firefighter. He'd also wanted to believe she wasn't a thief, but the fact that she, not Cass, had been the one insisting they go alone to the gallery had doused that hope.

She had to be worried her attacker would try again, yet she'd rather take that risk than bring him to her appointment. Had she figured out that he was FBI?

Probably not, or she'd have canceled the meeting for fear their plan had been compromised.

The guy hanging around the newspaper tent moved on, a young girl clutching his hand. The sisters posed with a giant brown bear outside the gift shop, feigning fear for their lives.

Sam winced at how believable their expressions looked. Had the attacks been staged, too? To lull him into thinking she wasn't involved? He shook away the ridiculous notion.

"Oh, man." Jake squeezed his shoulder. "You're really worried about her."

Sam jerked his gaze to Jake, and looked at him like he'd just landed from another planet.

"That came out wrong. Of course you are. We all are. And if you tried to join us at the Red Onion, Mom and Dad would likely turn you out on your ear."

The tour bus driver called for them to board. Once everyone had settled into their seat, he asked, "How'd you like Liarsville?"

"Loved it," Jen said cheerily, along with half the passengers.

He cringed at the connotation. She might not have lied about not knowing who tried to kill her, but she was definitely hiding something.

He reclined his seat, crossed his arms over his chest and pretended to sleep, hoping Jen and Cass would take advantage of their relative privacy to go over their plan to smuggle the stolen painting.

"I've decided to sell," Jen said in low tones.

Sam's ears perked at the news.

"Sell what?" Cass asked.

"My stake in the art gallery."

"You can't!"

"Shh." Jen stole a glance his way but was thankfully fooled by his not-quite-closed eyes. "You know how much I hate my identity being tied to it."

"Oh, c'mon. Reg apologized for bringing in the nude portraits. And hasn't brought in any since your complaint."

Huh. Sam's admiration for Jen regained a notch or two. Apparently she had some scruples.

"That's the least of my concerns."

Sam pursed his lips. Nix the scruples.

"Is this about Ian? Because he was a jerk. And selling the gallery won't spare you from lowlifes who are only interested in your money."

Sam clenched his fingers into a fist. He'd like to meet her ex-fiancé.

"It's not about Ian." Jen's voice sounded beyond weary. "I'm tired of living in the limelight."

"Well, I can't afford to buy you out and I don't want just anyone as my partner."

"What about selling your share, too? Think about it, Cass. You could do anything you want. Live anywhere you want."

"I like Seattle just fine."

Jen twisted her fingers in her lap, as if her desire

to get out of the gallery business was do or die. Did she know they were closing in? "Do you think you'll like it as well from a jail cell?"

Sam bit back a curse. Yeah, she knew. His pulse throbbed at his temples. She must've overheard his phone conversation on the balcony this morning. There was no way she would walk out of the Skagway gallery with the stolen painting.

Pretending to shift in his sleep, he half-turned toward the window and thumbed a text message to his team: Stand down.

A chilly mist hung over the town of Skagway, zapping Jennifer's courage. Or maybe it was the genuine concern in Sam's eyes when she'd again refused his offer to walk them to the gallery.

"It's only three blocks, Sam," she protested and flashed him a confident smile. "Pretty sure we can keep ourselves out of trouble."

"Not a river in sight," Cass added. "And we won't accept a drink from strangers."

"Oh!" Jennifer lifted a finger, signaling another thought. "And we'll look both ways before we cross the street."

"See that you do." Sam's stern tone made her jump.

Mrs. Steele patted Jen's arm. "He's only concerned for your welfare. He's not usually so bossy."

"Yes, he is," Jake quipped.

Sam shooed him into the Red Onion Saloon and caught her hand. The stroke of his thumb across the pulse point at her wrist sent a shiver of awareness up her arm. "Promise me you'll be careful."

"For crying out loud," Cass exclaimed. "Let him come with us if he's that worried. All this talk is starting to give me the willies."

Jennifer ignored her. "We'll be fine, Sam. We'll meet you back aboard for supper." She stiffened her spine and turned in the gallery's direction, praying for God's protection instead.

Cass had to jog a few steps to catch up. "I don't understand why you turned down his offer when yesterday you were going on about how much danger you'd been in. It's no wonder your boyfriends never last."

Jen stopped dead and faced her. "You don't? Really?"

"No. He seems to really care about you."

Jen resumed walking, this time at a faster clip. "We needed to finish our conversation."

"Oh, right. Your sister, the jailbird. Do you really think that poorly of me?" Cass lagged behind, scuffing her boots along the boardwalk. "What do you think—that I'll get thrown in jail for being drunk and disorderly at a gala?"

Jen spun on her heel and glared at her. "I know about the paintings, Cass."

"You know about what paintings?"

"Don't play games with me," Jen answered under her breath, prodding Cass forward. "I'm trying to give you an out. Save you from destroying your life."

Cass sloughed off Jen's hold. "I'm perfectly capable of taking care of myself."

Jennifer stopped at the street corner and squinted at her sister. Did she really not know about the paintings? Or was she just playing coy?

Jennifer ground her teeth in frustration and stepped off the curb.

Cass grabbed her arm and jerked her back as an old pickup sped by. "More capable than you, apparently."

They looked both ways and then crossed the street without incident. *"Look,"* Jennifer said. "There's no point in pussyfooting around the situation."

"No, by all means, jump right in. Tell me exactly what you think of me." Cass sounded hurt.

Jennifer looped her arm through her sister's. "Cass, I wasn't talking about your social life." She lowered her voice and spoke close to her ear. "I meant the stolen paintings."

"What paintings?" she shrieked.

"Shh." Jennifer tightened her grip on Cass's arm and forced her to keep walking. The wide sidewalks were packed with tourists from the two cruise ships docked in port. Some were just out to take in the sights of the old-fashioned-looking town. Most were being lulled into jewelry stores and T-shirt shops to lighten their wallets. Jennifer glanced around to make sure no one was watching them. "The paintings Uncle Reggie is apparently fencing."

"What? No way. You sure you didn't hit your head on a rock when you fell in the river?"

Her surprise seemed genuine, which lightened Jennifer's heart. The sun even peeked out from behind a cloud. "You had no idea?"

"Of course not. Because there's no way he'd do such a thing."

"There is. And he has. And if we don't get out now, he'll take us down with him." Jen glanced around, suddenly feeling like tourists on every side had eyes on them.

"You're crazy. Are you hearing yourself?"

Jennifer pulled Cass out of the flow of pedestrian traffic. "Can I borrow your phone?" Cass handed it over and Jen thumbed through the screens of the FBI database. When she found the image of *A Duel After the Masked Ball* that she'd spotted in the gallery's storage room, she showed it to Cass. "You recognize this?"

Cass squinted at the image. "I'm not sure."

"You should. It's in the gallery's storage room."

"O-kay."

Jennifer zoomed out the image on the screen. "And it's listed on the FBI's stolen art database."

Cass gasped. "There's no way Reg could've known."

"I wouldn't be so sure."

"How can you say that? He's always taken good care of us."

"Yeah." She glanced around at the stores hawking their wares to unsuspecting bargain hunters. "Clearly, we've been a lucrative occupation."

Cass let out another gasp.

Jennifer shoved the phone in her pocket and urged Cass to start walking again. "Let's see what he's arranged for us to pick up here in Skagway, shall we?"

"You think he'd ask us to smuggle a stolen painting?"

"That's exactly what I think."

"I don't believe it."

"We'll soon find out. And if I'm right, I hope you'll agree we should leave it behind and sell the gallery as soon as possible, ideally before Uncle Reggie learns we're on to him."

Cass's mouth opened and shut like the pet guppy they'd had as kids. For the first time since learning of Uncle Reggie's request, Jennifer hoped her suspicions were true.

As they stopped to cross the next street, Jennifer glanced over her shoulder and glimpsed a guy behind them duck into a store. Maybe it was just her overactive imagination, but she wasn't in the mood to take any chances.

"Let's go this way." She tugged Cass around the corner and down the side street to the next block before continuing in the direction they'd been traveling. The street was residential and quiet. Too quiet for her comfort. She glanced over her shoulder, but thankfully no one trailed them.

They turned up the next block and entered the gallery by the side door. The lighting was dim—uncomfortably so. Not what she'd expect in a gallery.

Except the art, if you could call it that, was as dark as the room.

"I don't see anything here that Uncle Reggie could possibly want for our gallery," Cass whispered.

"I doubt he plans to display whatever he's ordered."

An overgrown hippie with long scraggly gray hair appeared behind the counter. "May I help you?"

Jen noted the glance of a female tourist browsing at the front of the gallery and lowered her voice. "Uh, our uncle asked us to pick up his order—Reginald Michaels."

"Ah, yes, of course. I should have realized. You must be the Robbins twins."

"Yes."

He ambled to a back room and eventually returned with a wrapped package.

"We'll need to take it unwrapped to board the ship."

"Yes, of course. I wasn't thinking." His lack of concern worried Jennifer. If she was wrong about the piece being stolen, Cass would doubt her story altogether.

He opened the package and showed them the small gilt-framed ink drawing of a beautiful native woman—a drawing unlike anything else in the store.

Jennifer's hopes rose. "Oh, excuse me." She pretended to be responding to a text message on Cass's phone as she scanned the FBI's stolen art database. Cass, bless her heart, asked the painting's name and artist and age, speeding up the search. It wasn't on the database. Jennifer snapped shut the phone.

A knowing grin crept across Cass's lips. Victorious. Vindicated. Had she known Jennifer wouldn't find it? Had her shock over the allegations been a ruse?

"Are we good to go then?" Cass asked.

"Yes."

The curator wrapped the piece in padded paper and slipped it into a bag. The bell above the front door jangled. The female tourist left and a guy in a red Alaska jacket strolled in, stopping at a wall of masks near the front of the store. A second man she hadn't realized was in the store appeared at the back of the room.

The hair on Jen's neck prickled to attention. She grabbed Cass's arm. "C'mon, let's go." She opted to leave out the side door they'd come in, even though it opened onto a much less populated street.

Unfortunately, the street was downright empty. Or maybe not so unfortunate. She veered back to the residential street they'd detoured on earlier, rather than the busy street where they'd be expected.

"Hey," Cass protested. "Now that we've fulfilled our errand, I'd hoped to do some shopping." Cass dragged her back past the gallery, but surprisingly, she didn't breathe a word against Jennifer's earlier allegations.

Behind them, the gallery's side door slapped open.

"Run," Jen shouted, not caring how they must look. Better safe than sorry.

A guy lunged at them, ripping the package from Cass's hand. Cass kept on running for the safety of the crowded main street.

The guy kicked Jen's legs out from under her and she crashed to her knees. "Help!" she cried, but Cass had already disappeared into the noisy throng. Too noisy to hear her cry before a meaty hand clamped over her mouth. *Oh, God, please, I don't want to die.*

TEN

Sam stationed himself behind the moose T-shirts in the front window of the shop across the street from the gallery, his attention fixed on the gallery's door. His boss had refused to stand down the team, even without Sam in the picture to signal confirmation that the exchange involved the stolen painting.

Instead, the men tag-teamed acting as browsers in the gallery. *Whoa, wasn't that Monticello?* Sam shifted for a better view. He grabbed his phone to call it in as an undercover agent came out the shop door, cell phone in hand, calling him.

"You were right. The piece she took was a pen and ink, too small to conceal what we're after. She exited the store by the side entrance three minutes ago."

"Three minutes ago?" Sam raced toward the corner.

"Yeah, I hung around to make sure she didn't double back for the painting."

Sam hadn't seen the women emerge from the side street. But he hadn't exactly been watching for them from that direction, either. Ned should've notified him the instant she left the gallery.

Cass dashed into view, eyes wild, sleeve torn, hair flying.

Jen! Sam lurched on the curb and cut across behind the next car. Horns honked. Cass's gaze collided with his, relief instantly easing the panicked lines in her face.

He caught her by the upper arms. "Where's Jen?"

"Right behind—" She looked over her shoulder and the panic returned full force. "I don't know! This guy came out of nowhere, grabbed the package."

"Stay here."

Sam hit the side street in time to see Jen slam an impressive kick into the guy's kneecap. Then, squirming sideways in his loosened hold, she drew back her elbow, looking ready to drill a hand butt up his nose.

"Hey!" he shouted, racing toward them. "Let her go."

The guy flung her at Sam like a rag doll and hoofed it.

Sam caught Jen before she face-planted on the sidewalk. "You okay?" Finger impressions dented her cheeks.

"Yes! Go after him!"

He hesitated. Cass appeared at the end of the street, arms hugging her waist.

"I'm fine," Jen insisted.

"Wait with your sister." Sam took off after the guy who'd already veered out of sight. As Sam turned the corner, the guy tossed a package under a bush and slowed to a sedate pace, probably hoping to blend in. Sam sprinted to within ten feet of him before the guy shot a glance over his shoulder and picked up his pace.

Then a uniformed officer appeared at the next corner and the guy hesitated.

That's all the opportunity Sam needed to close the distance. He grabbed the guy's arm and wrenched it behind his back, bringing him to his knees. "You're under arrest for assault." Sam noted the guy's worn, brown leather lace-ups—the same kind worn by the guy he'd chased from her cabin. He had the same wiry build and dark hair, too. Had it been Jen's fear and an added disguise that made the guy seem hulking when he'd pushed her into the river? Or was there still another guy out there?

The officer relieved Sam of the scumbag and snapped on handcuffs as Sam retrieved the package the guy had tossed.

The officer shoved the suspect back the way they'd come. Outside the gallery's side door, Jen and Cass stood huddled around a second officer, who took their statements.

Cass's eyes lifted their way and she gasped. "You?"

Sam handed her the recovered package. "You know this guy?"

"He's the brother of one of the artists we've showcased." Her brow furrowed as she studied the guy. "Why?"

"Why else? I needed the money," he spat. "Not everyone is born with a silver spoon in their mouth."

Jen's head tilted, her expression intense, as if she was trying to match his voice or look or body language to the other attacks.

"You got ID?" the officer who'd been interrogating the twins asked the suspect.

"Sure. Back pocket."

The officer pulled a driver's license from the wallet. "Dwayne Bellamy of Seattle. You're a long way from home, Mr. Bellamy. How's someone so desperate for cash find himself in my neck of the woods?"

Bellamy's lips pressed together in a hard line.

"Were you on the cruise ship?" Sam pressed, certain he already knew the answer.

Bellamy didn't so much as acknowledge Sam's question with a glance. "I ain't answering any questions without my lawyer," he growled to the officer.

"That's your right." He motioned the officer holding Bellamy to load him into the patrol car.

"Is there a cruise card in his wallet?" Sam asked the officer.

He thumbed through the wallet and produced a card identical to the one Sam received upon boarding. "Yup. You got a reason for asking?"

Sam nodded toward Jen. "We're on the same ship, and Miss Robbins has been the victim of three prior incidents this trip."

"Thefts?" the officer asked Jen.

"No." Her voice came out mouselike. "Attacks."

"And you think that guy's behind them?"

Her gaze tracked to the police car the other officer had just shoved Bellamy into. "I'm not sure. His voice sounds like the waiter who gave me the drink, except the waiter had an accent. He's the same build, too."

Sam would love twenty minutes alone with the guy to find out, but that wasn't an option. He didn't recall the name from the list of people who'd been on their tour. But security would be able to determine if he'd been ashore at the time Jen was pushed into the river.

Jen rubbed at her arm. "I don't even know his brother. Why would he target me?"

"Sounds like he harbors a heap of resentment against rich folks." The officer's gaze surveyed Cass's stylish outfit, from her polished leather boots up to the diamond pendant hanging from her neck.

"This is crazy," Cass protested. "He was just after a quick buck. The drawing is worth a couple of grand."

"No!" Indignation blazed in Jen's eyes. "If that's all he wanted, he would've gotten away. He'd already snatched the drawing from you before he turned on me."

"You think he wanted the attack to look like a robbery gone bad?" the officer asked.

"She did receive a threatening note before leaving Seattle." Sam gave the officer the name of the detective investigating that case and of the detective on the assault in Juneau. "The ship leaves port in a few hours, so you'll want to have his cabin searched immediately. Question his travelling companion if he has one."

"Okay, we'll look into it."

The officer had clearly clued in that Sam was the FBI's undercover agent, but thankfully, Jen and Cass didn't seem to think it strange he'd take advice from "a friend of the victim."

"Do you need to see a doctor?" the officer asked Jen, eyeing the arm she was rubbing again.

"No, thanks. I'm fine. Now that you've arrested this guy, I can finally relax."

Sam moved to her side. Far from seeming fine, she looked haunted. He doubted nabbing Bellamy meant the threat was past. Whoever hired him was bound to have a backup plan. The best they could hope for was they'd choose to lay low until the heat was off.

"Thank you for not listening to me," she said.

"How do you mean?"

"Following us to make sure we were okay."

He brushed a thumb along the angry welt on her chin. "I was worried about you."

Her jaw stiffened, reminding him of Jake's comment about the female firefighter's pride. Jen may not be a *fire*fighter, but she had a lot of fight in her. "That was one impressive move you pulled on that guy. You a black belt?"

She hooked her thumbs through her belt loops, a smile playing on her lips. "No, just brown leather."

Chuckling, he grabbed his ringing cell phone— his FBI boss from Boston. "Excuse me a sec. I need to take this."

"What's going on?" Special Agent McEwan barked.

Sam filled him in on Dwayne Bellamy.

"Where's the painting *you* were sent to recover?"

"I don't know, sir." Sam reported seeing the guy who'd bought the auctioned painting.

"Well, why didn't you follow him?"

"Jennifer Robbins was being attacked."

"And it's the Skagway PD's job to protect her. Not yours. Have you forgotten what happened the last time you prioritized helping a woman over doing your job?"

"No, sir." Sam swallowed the bitter taste that always burned his throat at any reference to Lucy Carmichael, or Jezebel, as his brother preferred to call her. Sam's gaze strayed to Jen. The welt on her chin. The bruise on her arm. There was no way she set up the attack to distract him from seeing where the stolen painting really went, but that didn't mean someone hadn't.

He forwarded Sal Monticello's picture to his FBI counterpart. Maybe one of their agents noticed whether he acquired anything while in the store. Message sent, Sam returned to the group and offered to walk the twins back to the ship.

His stomach knotted at the thought that Jen would likely be dead by now if he hadn't befriended her this trip. Different jurisdictions. Different investigations. And if any one attack had succeeded, there was no one to alert authorities to the prior incidents, except for Cass.

Jen was looking less and less like a suspect, but could he trust her with the truth?

They passed the Red Onion Saloon with its bawdy

girls making eyes at any guy who happened by. An act—just like the feigned interest of the last woman he'd fallen for.

He couldn't afford to be wrong again.

Jennifer dragged her feet as Cass fell into step beside Sam heading back to the ship. She was shaky from the attack, could still feel where Bellamy's fingers had dug into her cheek.

Sam turned and waited for her to catch up, concern radiating from his gaze. As his hand moved protectively to the small of her back, she offered him a grateful smile...all the more grateful for his security experience. This afternoon could've turned out a lot differently if he hadn't shown up when he did.

But now that her attacker was in custody, she was more worried about what Cass might say to Uncle Reggie about their earlier conversation if she got the chance to call him before they set sail. They wouldn't return to Seattle for four days, and if he found out they—or at least she—suspected him of making illegal deals, he might clear out their trust accounts, skip the country and leave them with a worse scandal to deal with than if she'd gone straight to the police.

If only she hadn't said anything to Cass about her suspicions until after she'd verified whether the piece was stolen. Jen slanted a glance at her unusually quiet twin, an uncomfortable thought whispering through her mind. What if Cassie's skepticism about the allegations was an act?

Jen rubbed her still-sore arm. She'd been awfully

quick to dismiss the attack as nothing more than petty theft despite Bellamy's connection to their gallery.

As if Sam had read her thoughts, he asked, "Any reason Bellamy might have a grudge against the gallery?"

Cass shrugged. "Only if he's jealous of his brother's success. We've helped his brother make quite a name for himself."

They passed the railway, and Sam steered them toward a shortcut to the ship through the park. The quiet hush of the trees and their earthy pine scent soothed her frazzled nerves.

"You ever get the sense Bellamy was jealous?" Sam pressed Cass.

"No, he's never struck me as all that ambitious. He's done a few odd jobs for the gallery. Mostly, I think he lives off his brother's generosity."

Jen's pulse spiked yet again as she exchanged a glance with Sam. "What kind of jobs?"

"Pick ups and—" Cass wagged her finger. "Oh, no. You're not going to try to blame the attacks on Uncle Reggie, too."

"Too?" Sam quizzed.

Jen cringed. Dropping back a step to slip out of Sam's sight, she sliced her fingers across her throat to signal Cass to cut the commentary.

Cass ignored her. "Yeah, Jen has this crazy idea Reg—"

"Cass!" Jen gasped.

Cass rolled her eyes. "She thinks our guardian has been selling stolen art. She told me this—" Cass waved the wrapped pen and ink in front of Sam's face "—was likely stolen. Which it *isn't*."

Jen's next breath came out strangled. "Cass, I'm sure Sam doesn't want to hear about our business problems."

Cass walked backward on the path ahead of them and fluttered a hand at Jen's protest, as if the entire conversation were a lark. "I'm sure he doesn't care. Do you care, Sam?"

Sam didn't answer right away, and as they descended the hill toward the ship, the mist seemed to close in around them. How could Cass tell him? If he mentioned her suspicions to the detective, the police would investigate them as a possible motive for Bellamy's attacks, and…okay, they probably were. And…and…maybe Bellamy wasn't acting alone. Maybe Uncle Reggie or one of his cohorts paid him to come after her. And…

Her stomach churned. And maybe this wasn't over. Maybe they'd send someone else to try again.

Sam closed his hand over hers. "I'd like to help, if I can. I might be able to help you see the pieces of the puzzle you're missing or set a trap to catch your guardian in the act."

A glimmer of hope lifted her spirits. "Without involving the police?"

Sam's steps slowed. He tilted his head, his expression inscrutable. "Why wouldn't you want to involve the police?"

She nibbled her bottom lip, wishing the ground

would open and swallow her on the spot. What must he think of her?

"Are you afraid you'll be implicated, too?"

Her eyes shot wide open. "No! I don't even work there." Her gaze slid to Cass.

"Your sister or your uncle then?"

"Oh, brother," Cass moaned. "Don't encourage her. Reg loves us like his own daughters. She's probably more worried about word leaking out to the newspapers."

"Cass!"

"It's true. You don't care a fig about what happens to Reg." Cass plucked a leaf off a tree lining the path, scrunched it, then, thrusting it toward Jen, let it tumble to the ground. "If you did, you wouldn't be trying to sell out from under him with all he's done for us."

"That's not true. I appreciate that he took us in and managed the gallery so well." A couple passed them on the path and Jen lowered her voice. "If I didn't, don't you think I would have called the police the second I found the stolen painting in the back room?"

"Right, that's why your face lit when Sam offered to help you trap Reg."

"It's not the way you make it sound!"

"No, because an investigation into allegations of theft would make selling next to impossible." Cass spun on her heel and flounced off ahead of them.

"Jen." Sam caught her arm, his tone urgent. "If you've found a stolen painting, we need to report it. If you try to cover for your uncle and the police find out, you could be charged with aiding and abetting."

She squirmed. Why did Cass have to bring all this up in front of him? She obviously wasn't involved in whatever Uncle Reggie was up to or she would have kept her mouth shut. That was one good thing at least. But unless Jen could convince her that Uncle Reggie was crooked, it didn't look as though she'd ever agree to sell. Or worse, if all this hit the fan, no buyer would want to purchase it.

"She didn't find a stolen painting." Cass resumed her backward walk. "It was probably a reproduction. Art students do that sort of thing all the time to develop their skills. Some are really good at it. Reggie's bought a few. But he's never tried to pass them off as the real thing."

Sam squeezed Jen's hand. "Could that painting have been a reproduction?"

"Maybe, but I didn't think so."

His brow furrowed. "Did you intend to let Reg get away with the thefts?"

The censure in his voice niggled at her conscience. "I don't want to. I mean, I know the victims deserve to get their property back, but..."

They reached the pier, and the ship that had seemed so small from the top of the hill now felt massive—like the theft she'd wanted to ignore. "I just wanted out," she moaned. "If Uncle Reggie's actions go public, no one will believe that Cass and I didn't know."

Sam stopped walking and clasped Jen's upper arms. His gaze fell to her hand nervously rubbing the cross at her throat. "Better to be maligned unfairly than to compromise your faith to avoid it."

She dropped her hand to her side. *He was right.* Deep down she'd felt her conscience pricking her from the moment she'd found the stolen painting. But the thought of the press latching on to the story terrified her. Their scrutiny after her parents' accident had been brutal.

"Oh, great," Cass complained at the sight of a crowd milling around two police cars parked alongside the ship.

"There they are," a man shouted and rushed toward them, followed by a man with a news camera.

No. The air burned Jen's lungs. How'd they find them?

A blonde in a chic blue skirt suit shoved a microphone into Jen's face. "Are you Jennifer Robbins?"

Jen shot Sam a desperate look.

Sam hooked his arm through hers and, holding out his other arm, ramrodded through the gawkers. "Miss Robbins doesn't wish to comment."

Cass hurried along on Jen's other side.

The woman clattered after them in her three-inch heels. "Who are you? And what is your connection to Jennifer Robbins?"

"No comment," Sam muttered as more people poured around them.

The tenacious reporter got ahead of them with her cameraman. "But we've learned this isn't the first attack against Miss Robbins. Do you believe they're connected to rumors the Robbins Gallery is brokering stolen art?"

Jen froze. This couldn't be happening.

Cass pushed past her. "Where did you hear such ridiculous nonsense?"

"We received a tip from a reliable source."

Cass snorted. "Yeah, if I had a nickel for every time I've heard that."

Sam's gaze shot to a man standing near one of the police cars.

Jen's heart jerked at the vehemence there. Did Sam suspect one of the investigators of leaking information?

The muscles in his arms and jaw tensed with barely concealed rage as he fixed his glare back on the blonde. "Reginald Michaels manages the gallery on behalf of the Robbinses. Any questions you have about deals should be directed to him."

"We tried. But he's missing."

Jen's heart climbed to her throat. "What—" She swallowed and tried again. "What do you mean missing?"

ELEVEN

Sam helped Jen and Cass escape the press only to be cornered by the investigators aboard the ship. He managed to extricate the twins from the probing about what was found in Bellamy's room fairly quickly and, after walking Jen and Cass to their cabin to rest before dinner, he stormed back to the meeting room where he'd left his fellow FBI agent.

"Why am I only hearing about Reginald Michaels's disappearance from a news reporter twenty-four hours after the fact?" She'd said he'd closed the gallery early yesterday afternoon—timing uncomfortably coincidental to Jen's plunge in the river—and hadn't been seen or heard from since.

"We only found out about it minutes before you." The harsh edge to the older agent's tone left no doubt who he blamed for failing to recover the stolen painting. But clearly, more was going on here than they'd anticipated.

Sam drilled him with a glare. "You were supposed to be searching Bellamy's cabin for evidence he was behind the other attacks against her. So what's with giving Jen the third degree over the printout you found in his room of the gallery's acquisitions and disbursements?"

"If it was stolen from her cabin, as she claims now, why didn't she report it missing at the time?"

"She told you. She didn't realize the papers were gone. When did she go from being a victim to being a suspect?"

The agent's eyes narrowed. "She's been a suspect from day one. Something *you* seem to have forgotten."

"For your information, a few moments before your news reporter made a circus out of this investigation, Jennifer Robbins revealed to me her discovery of the stolen *A Duel After the Masked Ball* and her suspicions of her former guardian." Sam held his thumb and forefinger a quarter inch apart and thrust them toward the agent's face. "And I was this close to convincing her to work with the police to bring him down."

He clenched his jaw at the thought of how she'd intended to cover for her thieving "uncle" by quietly selling the gallery. Was it out of a misplaced sense of loyalty? Or purely out of self-interest, as Cass had implied?

Sam shook off the thought. Based on how Jen had cowered at the press's onslaught, she'd done it out of self-preservation. Cass was another story. He wasn't so sure her supposed ignorance of the theft wasn't an act to throw him and Jen off.

"For your information—" the FBI agent's gaze

veered to the ship's window "—we didn't sic the news reporter on the women."

"Then I hope you've confiscated that cameraman's tape because if they run it and someone tips them off to my real identity—"

"Taken care of."

Sam nodded his appreciation. "Have you located Bellamy's roommate?"

"Still looking." The agent handed him a picture. "She's aboard the ship somewhere. We also found pills that could be Rohypnol in Bellamy's shaving kit. We'll have them tested and let you know what we find out."

Sam studied the woman's picture. "Is her name on the list of people who bought soft drinks the first night?"

"Yes, at the bar nearest the casino—a floor down from the art gallery. So she could have supplied it to Bellamy."

"Any calls made to or from the room?"

"Nope. And Bellamy claims he doesn't own a cell phone. We're looking into it. You got a theory?"

"Yeah. Michaels might've figured out Jen was on to him, or is planning to sell the gallery, or both, and hired Bellamy to get rid of her and make it look like an unlucky tourist incident." Sam folded the picture of Bellamy's roommate into his pocket. "Michaels probably never intended for the women to make it to the gallery. Did your men track down Monticello?"

"Yeah," the agent barked, clearly irritated that Sam hadn't alerted him to the man sooner. Not that Sam blamed him. The local feds were singularly interested in recovering the stolen painting, not in helping Sam haul in the larger net he'd cast. "We checked his packages when they returned to the ship. No painting. We're checking what security camera footage we can to track his movements after leaving the gallery."

"And turn up the heat on Bellamy. Michaels likely skipped the country after hearing Jennifer survived being pushed into the river, afraid Bellamy would give him up. If Bellamy learns his cash flow has dried up, maybe he'll start talking."

The agent bobbed his head from side to side as if the theory didn't jibe. Or maybe he was just irritated that none of this would help him locate the missing painting. "We're checking flights, got a BOLO on Michaels's car, but his credit card was clean. No charges on it since he disappeared yesterday afternoon."

"Talk to his son?"

"Not yet, but the background check you requested on him came back clean."

"Okay." Sam blew out a breath. "So do we think someone took Reg out?"

"Haven't found any evidence of it, but if he's mixed up with the mob, who knows?"

Yeah, Sam needed to seal Jennifer's trust and figure out what was really going on in the Robbins Gallery before it was too late.

"You two get your picture taken." Cass pushed Jen and Sam toward the backdrop the ship's professional photographer had set up in the wide hall.

"That's okay," Jen said when the photographer turned eager eyes their way. From how adamantly Sam had resisted his mom's attempts to get him in on the family picture, he clearly didn't like the idea of his picture on display for the rest of the passengers to see.

Sam's mother motioned to a second backdrop the photographer wasn't using. "Stand over here then."

To Jen's surprise, Sam obliged. It was another formal night and he looked heart-stutteringly gorgeous in a black tux in front of the glacier-blue backdrop.

He lifted his hand toward her. "I promise not to bite."

Jake gave her a little push. Sam caught her hand and whirled her to his side as Sam's mom and Cass snapped photos.

"Hey, I wasn't smiling."

"The gentleman was smiling enough for the both of you." The professional photographer stepped forward and positioned their hands and chins into a formal pose.

"Oh, we really don't—"

Mrs. Steele caught the photographer's arm and pointed him to a couple eagerly waiting for him at the other backdrop. "Have I told you how beautiful you look tonight?" Sam whispered close to Jen's ear, his breath lifting the wisps escaping her updo.

"No talking," Cass said, her gaze on her camera screen, her finger continuously clicking the button.

Tommy bounced up and down, tugging on his father's arm. "Hurry. We're going to miss the show."

Cass lowered her camera. "All done."

Sam's mom and dad strolled ahead of them looking every bit as in love as they probably had on their wedding day, forty years ago tonight.

Jen was glad Sam had talked her out of hiding in her cabin all night. After being sideswiped by that reporter's questions, she hadn't felt up to celebrating. And it hadn't helped that they'd had no better success than the reporter in tracking Reggie down by phone. Cass had managed to get hold of his son, Blake, who'd tried to reassure her that his father had probably had an opportunity for a sweet deal and took off without thinking to leave word. Of course, the kind of sweet deal that would lure him away was what worried Jen. But thankfully Cass didn't blabber about Jen's suspicions the way she had to Sam, just about the reporter's fishing expedition.

Blake had promised to try to find his father and do what damage control he could. Their aunt Martha, however, was more reticent. Not that they'd expected her to know where Reggie was; the couple had divorced soon after Jen and Cass left for college. But her warnings to be careful suggested she knew more than she was saying.

Jen refocused on Sam's much-happier parents. When she and Cass added their voices to Sam and Jake's "Happy Anniversary" song at dinner, she'd been transported back to long-ago celebrations with their own parents. Mom and Dad had been so in love, too. If only she and Cass could be as fortunate to find men who would love them for themselves, not their money or status.

Sam twined his fingers between hers. "Penny for your thoughts."

"I was just thinking how happy your parents look and remembering my own."

"I wish they could be here for your and Cassie's birthday celebration."

The sincerity in his voice squeezed her chest, making her forget all the reasons why she shouldn't be letting her heart turn somersaults around him. "Having your family celebrate with us will make it very special." And having those pictures would be a bittersweet reminder of how special.

Spotting the ladies' room outside the lounge where the comedic magician would be performing, she quickly excused herself.

Cass trailed her in and grinned at Jen's reflection. "You'll thank me later when you see the great shots I got of you two."

"I can't believe you did that to me."

Cass elbowed Jen's arm. "Oh, c'mon, why not? You like him, don't you?"

"That's not the point. He lives on the other side of the country." Jen dug in her purse for her lip gloss, trying not to think about how much she'd miss Sam after this trip.

"Oh, brother, Jen. People can change jobs. Move. Don't blow this before you take the time to see if you two could be more than a shipboard romance."

"This from the self-proclaimed fling queen."

"Hey, I'm totally up-front with guys about what I'm in a relationship for. You're the one who's a bundle of mixed messages."

Jen glared at her sister's reflection. "I am not."

Cass quirked an eyebrow.

Jen gave up on finding the lip gloss and spun toward Cass. "You'd be a mess, too, if you'd been drugged, half-drowned and dragged out by some lunatic who has it in for rich women."

Cass's grin instantly fell. "You're right. I'm sorry. I was just trying to help."

Jen worried her bottom lip. If Cass really wanted to help, she'd agree to sell her half of the gallery. But Jen bit back the urge to say so. They were celebrating the Steeles' anniversary tonight. Family arguments could wait until morning. "We'd better get back."

Sam stood alone in the hallway. The appreciative glint in his eye, as they emerged, warmed her cheeks.

Oh, boy, she seriously needed to start pulling away before her heart got any more entangled. "Did the others go in already?"

"Yeah. I asked them to save us seats. They were filling up fast." He rested his palm at the small of her back. But instead of sending her stomach into another somersault routine, his touch silenced her frazzled thoughts, which should've unnerved her even more.

The two-story arena, with its second level a wide balcony overlooking the stage, had subdued lighting and leather-upholstered chairs flanking small tables, giving it a definite "lounge" feel—a place for adults. "Are you sure this show will be appropriate for Tommy?"

"I hope so. It's billed as family friendly and the kid's been keyed up about seeing it ever since he saw the poster on the announcement board."

Jake stood in the center of the room and waved them over. Cass must've taken to heart their discussion in the ladies' room, because rather than taking the empty seat next to Jake she sat in one of the pair of empty ones, leaving no way for Jen to sit next to Sam without someone else moving.

Disappointment flickered over Sam's brow, but he took the seat beside his brother without comment.

The cruise director introduced tonight's talent as coming all the way from Florida, after which the man took a bow at center stage and swept off his top hat. A dove flew out and Tommy clapped wildly.

"*Florida.* Imagine how much this guy has to travel," Jen said to the table in general. "I don't think I could stand that."

"Me, either." Mrs. Steele patted her son's hand. "We don't get to see Sam nearly as much as we'd like because of his job."

"Any chance you'd ever settle back in the Seattle area, *Sam?*" Cass asked with a practiced innocence Jen recognized all too well.

"Cass." She kicked her sister in the ankle.

Sam's melt-in-your-mouth chocolate-brown eyes came to rest on Jen. "It's possible."

Jake snorted. "That's what they say about world peace too."

Sam shot his brother a sideways look. Jen couldn't see it, but there was no mistaking the pop in the muscle in his cheek. He clearly didn't appreciate his brother's commentary.

Jake held up his hands in innocence. "I just call 'em like I see 'em."

Sam's mother squeezed his hand. "It would be wonderful to have you home again."

Sam's smile didn't reach his eyes, as if maybe more than his job kept him away. Yet he'd intimated that with the right incentive he might move back. An incentive like her?

She dropped her gaze to her soda glass. Did she want to be an incentive?

She enjoyed spending time with the Steeles, would miss them terribly when the cruise ended. They were so warm and gracious and everything she longed for in a family. And Sam… He was thoughtful and protective and seemed to take a genuine interest in her. *Her,* not her bank account.

Of course, she'd been fooled before. She watched Sam scoop Tommy into his lap, giving his nephew a better view of the stage. He grinned at the boy's excitement and tousled his hair affectionately. No, Sam was nothing like Ian.

A low vibration sound snagged Sam's attention to his pocket. He checked the screen on his phone, then set Tommy on his chair. "It's the Skagway police department. I asked them to call if they had any news. Excuse me. I'll step into the hall to take this where it's quiet."

Mrs. Steele patted Jen's clasped hands, drawing attention to her white knuckles. "Why don't you go with him? I'm sure you're anxious to hear the report."

"Yes. Excuse me." She found Sam standing next to one of the windows that lined the wide hall. He looked out at the water, listening intently to whoever was on the other end of the phone. She touched his elbow so he'd know she was there but couldn't read his expression to know if the news was good.

What seemed like an eternity later, he finally turned off his phone.

"What'd they say?"

"They confirmed the pills they found in Bellamy's shaving kit were roofies."

Her breath swept from her lungs in utter relief. "So I can stop worrying about everything I eat or drink. Did he confess to pushing me into the river, too?"

The muscles in Sam's jaw tensed. They did that a lot, she'd noticed, when he had to tell her something he'd rather not. "He hasn't confessed to anything. But the ship's card-scanning software confirmed he was off the ship at the time. There were no charges to his credit card, however, to confirm his whereabouts."

"So they still have no idea why he targeted me?" Shivering, she hugged herself, wishing she'd brought a wrap.

"No, I'm sorry. The detective in Seattle is interrogating his brother. Hopefully he can shed some light on the situation."

"I don't get it. If Bellamy's so hard up for cash, how'd he afford the cruise?"

"Apparently his lady friend sprang for it after she'd had a rewarding night with him at the casino just outside Seattle. She said she thought he was her lucky charm. But he hasn't proved so lucky for her this trip. She's already racked up a couple thousand in losses at the onboard casino."

Jen's throat instantly dried. "Is she still aboard? Did she know what he was up to?"

"She claimed not." Sam turned his phone over and over in his hand, as if he wasn't convinced, or...

"The police didn't let Bellamy go, did they?"

"No. *No,*" Sam repeated, as if suddenly realizing his edgy movements had roused the fear. He caught her hand. "He's been flown to a correctional facility in Juneau to await his bail hearing."

"So if he makes bail, he could be back?" She hated the quiver in her voice.

"The captain has banned him from reboarding. Besides, we're cruising Glacier Bay tomorrow and won't stop at another port until Ketchikan the morning after." At her relieved sigh, Sam rubbed her upper arms. "When the detective asked you about the papers in Bellamy's room, why didn't you tell him about the stolen painting you found at your gallery?"

"I was scared. You saw what vultures the reporters become when circling for a story."

Sam's gaze radiated compassion. "I want to help you."

"And I appreciate that. I appreciate that you didn't force my hand this afternoon."

An emotion she couldn't read flickered in his eyes

as his hands slipped from her arms. "Those reporter's questions aren't going to go away."

"Why do you care so much, Sam?"

That muscle in his jaw started working again. "You don't deserve what's been happening to you."

Her heart grew strangely heavy at his answer. They'd known each other less than two weeks. She lifted her chin. What had she expected him to say?

Because I care about you. Yeah, she would have liked to hear him say that. It had been a long, long time since she'd felt like anyone cared what happened to her.

Sam whisked his thumb across her cheek. Her *wet* cheek.

Mortified, she swiped at her eyes.

He cupped her face in his hands. "And because I care about you, Jen."

Tears clogged her throat at his tender declaration. *Oh, Lord, please don't let it be just a line he pulled out of his hat to entertain me like the magician back there.*

Their gazes tangled. His head dipped closer, his gaze not letting go of hers. Then his eyes slipped shut an instant before his lips found hers. Soft, gentle. His fingers glided through her hair and cradled her neck.

She slipped her arms around his waist. This must be what it felt like to be cherished.

Slowly, tentatively, he deepened the kiss. He tasted like chocolate and mint and…like she'd finally come home.

"Jenny and Sam sitting in a tree, K-I-S-S-I-N-G..." Tommy singsonged.

They sprang apart, her cheeks blazing.

His parents laughed as Jake cupped his hand over his son's mouth, and Cass, in her usual fashion, cried, "Way to go, Jen!"

But the daggers Jake glared at Sam betrayed a different sentiment.

And Jen's heart lodged in her throat for a whole different reason.

"You've sunk to new lows," Jake growled after tucking his sleeping son into bed.

"Save the lecture." Sam grabbed his toothbrush and locked himself in the bathroom. He felt sick enough about kissing Jen. He didn't need to hear what a jerk he was from his brother, too.

"She's not like Cass," Jake said through the door. "You can tell by the way she looks at you, at all of us, that this is no fling to her."

Sam jerked the door open. "What makes you think that's how I see it?"

"Oh, c'mon, you and I both know you'll never leave Boston. Not unless they throw you out."

Which they'd do in a heartbeat if he didn't fix this. Sam shoved his toothbrush back into his bag. He should be thankful Jake didn't know just how low he'd sunk. "You're telling me you've never been caught up in a moment and done something stupid?"

"So you admit it was stupid?"

"Yes. You happy?" He stalked to his bed and

yanked down the sheets. And all he could think about was how much he wanted to kiss her again. His suspect. Not that he suspected her anymore. Which should be worrying him a whole lot more.

"So what are you going to do about it?"

"I don't know."

"Mom will *kill* you if you break Jen's heart. The whole family is already halfway in love with her. She's amazing."

"I know she's amazing." Sam scrunched his pillow into a hard ball. "I'm the one who was kissing her. Remember?"

Tommy stirred at Sam's raised voice. He and Jake stilled. Once Tommy's breath evened out, Jake went on more quietly, "Is she safe now, at least? That guy's still locked up, isn't he?"

"Yeah, for now."

Jake gulped a swig of water from the bottle in the minifridge. "You still think their uncle hired the guy?"

Sam stared at the wall that separated their room from Jen and Cass's, not wanting to entertain the alternative—that Cass had. But she was the only one who'd benefit from Jen's death. "I don't know."

"Well, I don't care what intel you're supposed to be sweet-talking out of her. You can't keep leading Jen on if you don't mean it."

Sam rolled over, turning his back on his brother. "I don't want to talk about it."

"Fine, sleep. But take it from a firefighter—you're

playing with fire and if you don't wise up, the bad guy you're chasing isn't the only one who's going to get burned."

TWELVE

Jen's shy smile at breakfast the next morning made Sam feel slimier than seaweed. Last night, he'd simply been trying to take away the pain he'd seen in her eyes, the hurt she'd tried to hide with that defiant chin, unaware of the tears that had leaked from her eyes after his lame response to her question. He'd hated himself for putting them there, especially when he *did* care. And he couldn't deny feeling a little proud at Cass's rousing cheer and his parents' delighted laughter at finding him and Jen kissing.

"Did you see?" Jake jabbed his elbow into Sam's arm.

"Ow." Sam rubbed his bruised muscle. "See what?"

"The whale." Jake pointed to the window in front of their table, where their parents, Jen, Cass and Tommy were peering at the Icy Strait.

"Kind of like trying to spot the Loch Ness monster, I guess."

"There it is!" Tommy pointed to a spot much farther than where they'd been looking. His mom focused on it with her binoculars. Cass zoomed in with her camera.

Sam squinted but couldn't make out what had them all so excited. "I guess you need a pair of binoculars to get a good look at them from this height. What are we? Ten decks above the water?"

"It's still exciting," Cass gushed, her gaze fixed on the water.

"Yeah," Jake said. "Sometimes you get a better perspective if you look at the *big* picture."

"No." Cass pushed her camera screen in front of his face before Sam could counter Jake's needling. "See. Zoomed in you can see them really well, but when you zoom out they're just a speck." She shifted the camera in Sam's direction.

"You're right, just a *speck*." He emphasized the last word for Jake's benefit.

"Only we both know it's not," Jake grunted. "It's a four-ton killer whale."

Sam shoveled a forkful of eggs into his mouth. What did Jake expect him to do? Back off and tell Jen he'd made a mistake kissing her? That he couldn't see himself leaving his job any time soon and that it wasn't fair to lead her on? He didn't need three years of college psychology classes to know how that would go over. And right now, he couldn't risk alienating her.

"What's wrong, honey?" Sam's mother handed her binoculars to his dad and returned to her breakfast. "Didn't you sleep well?"

"Not great, no." Leave it to his mom to give him

an out for being a grouch this morning. He'd spent the night evaluating his options and not liking them. The truth was, he wanted to come clean, admit he was an FBI agent and ask Jen flat out to help him. But besides not being 100 percent sure he could trust her, and even less sure she'd agree, he was 99 percent sure she wouldn't keep the revelation from her sister. She was too desperate to convince Cass that Reginald Michaels was a criminal so she'd agree to sell the gallery. And what better way to prove it than to produce the FBI agent investigating him?

Trouble was Sam wasn't nearly as confident as Jen that her sister was innocent.

Another enthusiastic cry went up on the opposite side of the dining area, this time for an entire pod of whales.

Cass hurried back to the table and grabbed her coat. "I need to go out on deck for a better view. Anyone with me?"

Jen glanced his way as if to say, *Are we?*

Sam downed the last of his coffee and pushed his plate away. "Sure." What else could he do? The other options weren't really options. He had to continue the relationship as it was. The closer Jen felt to him, the more she'd trust him. He'd just have to try not to be left alone with her so there'd be no more kissing opportunities. A crowded deck sounded perfect.

But when her fingers laced trustingly through his, he hated himself for the necessary deception. He was no better than the woman who'd used *him*. Maybe worse.

* * *

Above the Icy Strait, gray clouds piled in the sky, blocking the sun's warming rays.

Jen stuffed her hands in her parka pockets and dipped her chin into the collar. "Wow, it's cold out here."

Sam tipped up her hood and gave her a sideways hug. "Being surrounded by icy water will do that."

Savoring the spicy fragrance of his cologne, she could think of a better way for Sam to warm her up, but he didn't seem eager to repeat last night's kiss. Hopefully he was just too self-conscious after Tommy's little serenade and not regretful it had happened.

She was glad Cass had talked her out of her sudden reservations after the kiss. Sam wasn't anything like Ian, who only feigned interest in her to get ahead. If anything, she was the one who'd benefited from their connection, with all his security know-how. And the fact he hadn't pushed her yesterday afternoon to tell the police her suspicions proved to her where his loyalties lay.

"Tommy and I are heading to the play area for a while," Jake said, holding Tommy by the hand. "A four year old can only handle watching the passing scenery for so long."

"We'll join you inside," Sam's mom said. "I could use a hot chocolate."

"You want to go in, too?" Sam asked Jennifer.

"Not yet." Last night he'd said he wanted to help her, and with how fast her plan to convince Cass to sell had unraveled, she needed all the help she could get. But she didn't want to talk to him in front of his family. Sam might not think less of her for not going straight to the police, but she cringed to think what his father—as a former sheriff—would think.

Cass turned off her camera. "I'm going to head in for a bit, too. See you later."

"You sure you don't want to go in, Jen? You're shivering." Sam held her a little closer, eliciting a dark look from Jake before he strode off.

"Why doesn't Jake want you hugging me?"

Sam laughed. "You noticed that, huh?"

"Kind of hard to miss."

"He likes you."

Her heart stuttered. "But I've never given him any reason to—"

"It's okay. Not that way." Sam's arms slipped from around her as sadness crept into his eyes. "He's afraid you'll be hurt when I go back to Boston."

The stark finality of his words sucked the air from her lungs. She rested her forearms on the ship's rail and gazed out over the barren ice fields—kind of how her future suddenly felt. Not that he'd led her on. "I had no expectations you'd stay. Boston's where your job is."

"Yeah," he said with a heavy breath.

"I guess you get tired of your family's subtle pressure to move closer to home."

He chuckled. "Subtle?"

"Hey, you're lucky to have them." Her voice cracked and she ducked her head.

"I am." Sam cupped her cheek. "And I don't think I realized how lucky until I saw them through your eyes."

Yearnings she shouldn't be entertaining stirred inside her at the warmth of his touch, the tenderness of his words. She turned back to the ship's railing, welcoming the sting of the cool air at the spot where his hand had been. "I spent a lot of years being mad at my parents for dragging us to the city, and maybe because I blamed the gallery for getting them killed, or maybe because being mad helped me to not miss them so much. But being with your family has reminded me of all the wonderful times we'd shared, too."

"I'm glad." Sam hugged her to his side once again.

Jen savored the comforting feel of his strong arm curled around her shoulders. For a long while they simply watched the passing scenery in silence, which was occasionally broken by the cry of gulls overhead. Surrounded by nothing but ice and water and sky, she could almost forget that someone had been trying to kill her, and that her uncle was missing, and that her hopes of quietly selling the gallery were doomed.

"How'd you end up in Boston?" she asked.

Sam's arm slipped from her shoulder. "Why do you ask?"

"If the questions that reporter threw at me yesterday are a taste of what's to come, I might need to hightail it there myself."

"Jen, the sooner you tell the police everything you know, the less likely this will all blow up in your face."

"But I don't really know anything. The guy who made me the offer on the gallery warned me to finalize the sale quickly and quietly because he claimed he'd heard that Uncle Reggie was mixed up with a shady character, and if word got out and damaged the gallery's reputation, then the deal was off." Jen hugged her waist. "I thought it was all hot air. That he was just trying to intimidate me...until I found that painting in the back room."

"The police will want to know the buyer's name so they can question him about where he got his information, and they'll want permission to search the gallery for other possible stolen pieces."

"I checked them all. That was the only one. And Cass is convinced that it's a reproduction. She thinks that reporter must've overheard us talking on the way to the gallery yesterday, and then after the attack, she figured she'd sensationalize the story."

"What about the buyer? Who is he? How's he know who your uncle's mixed up with? Are you sure you can trust him?"

"No. I'm not sure of anything. All I know is that he offered a fair price for the business and whole-sale value for every painting in inventory. His name is David Willis."

"What about that paperwork Bellamy stole from your room? Were you really just tabulating the inventory to prepare for selling the gallery like you told the police?"

She ducked her head. "No. I was going to check the items against the FBI's database."

He took her hand and tugged her away from the rail. "Well, let's start with that. Because the fact Bellamy stole the paperwork suggests it contained something incriminating."

"But how would he know?"

Sam ushered her inside and steered her to the elevator. "Given your uncle's disappearance, it seems pretty clear he found out about your suspicions and hired Bellamy to silence you. Then he skipped town when it looked like he might be exposed."

Her insides heaved. She hugged her middle again. "No. He might be corrupt, but he'd never sink that low. I'm like a daughter to him."

Inside the elevator, Sam tapped eight for their deck. "Are you sure?"

She chewed her bottom lip. "Not one hundred percent." Three weeks ago she'd never have believed him capable of selling stolen paintings. But did she really know him? She hadn't lived under his roof for more than five years.

"Then I suggest we check your gallery and trust accounts and whatever other assets he might have spirited away."

Her stomach bottomed out. "You think we could have lost everything?"

"Let's not borrow trouble." The elevator dinged, and Sam followed her out of the elevator and along the corridor toward her cabin. "Gather all the paperwork and account numbers you have, and we'll go to the internet café and see what we can find."

Jen shed her parka, and as Sam slipped into his own cabin to do the same, she quickly grabbed her purse and the paperwork the police had returned to her. Her gaze fell to the Bible she'd set on her nightstand the day they'd arrived and hadn't looked at since. She dumped everything she'd gathered onto the bed and, sinking to the floor, picked up the Bible. *Lord, please don't let Uncle Reggie have run off with all our money. Please let us be wrong about him.*

The Bible fell open to First Peter. "In His great mercy He has given us new birth into a living hope…" she read aloud. "Into an inheritance that can never perish, spoil or fade."

Her conscience pricked. All these years she'd lamented men only being interested in her wealth, and here she'd valued it more than doing the right thing. Well, it and sparing Cass and herself from being falsely branded again. She remembered all too well how lonely a path that was to walk.

She squeezed her eyes shut and hugged the Bible to her chest. "Thank you for protecting me from Bellamy and for bringing Sam into my life to help me through this."

Something rustled behind her.

She sprang to her feet, the Bible spilling to the floor, knocking Cass's novel from the nightstand. "Sam, I didn't hear you come in."

The soft look in his eyes made her heart flutter.

"I was just—" She waved her hand toward the floor.

A smile whispered over his lips. "I heard." He picked up the Bible and the novel. His head tilted, a frown replacing his smile. He reached between the nightstand and trash can, where the novel had fallen, and picked up a business card. "Is this yours?" He passed her what was actually a gift card.

"Enjoy your trip. Can't wait for our *own* celebration," she read, then glanced at the back, looking for a signature. There wasn't one. "I've never seen this before." She honed in on the word *own,* and an uneasy feeling rippled through her stomach at what they might have planned to celebrate.

Sam's heart twisted at the sight of Jen's fingers trembling over the keyboard in the internet café. The note he'd found—the note Cass had kept from Jen—had left her shaken. As they'd walked to the computer area, he'd tried to reassure her that it could be innocent, that maybe Cass didn't want her to know she had a new love interest, but Jen hadn't looked as if she believed it any more than he did.

"The trust accounts are intact," Jen reported, her voice regaining a little energy. She exited the bank's website, cleared the system's cache and then logged into another. "The gallery's bank is asking for password verification because I'm on a computer it doesn't recognize."

"What's the question?"

"What's your mother's maiden name? But my mother's didn't work."

"Do you know Reginald's?"

"Not a clue."

"Okay, just a sec." Pretending to do an internet search on his phone, he texted the Seattle FBI office and asked. After receiving their response, he told Jen, "Try Friesen."

Jen typed. "Yes, we're in. How'd you figure that out so fast?"

"Family tree dot com." Sam winked and hunkered down beside her. "No large withdrawals have been made." Sam's chest tightened. This wasn't necessarily good. If Michaels wasn't using credit cards and hadn't cleaned out the accounts, chances were he wasn't flying off to havens unknown. Chances were he'd run into foul play, the same as Jen. "We need to talk to Cass."

"But we haven't checked the paintings on the list yet." Jen's tone had naïvely brightened at finding no evidence her uncle had defrauded their trust fund.

"Right, give me a page and I'll work on a second computer so we can go through them quickly." As Sam waited for the database to load, he texted their latest findings to the Seattle office and renewed his request that they track down who sent the gift basket to the twins.

His thoughts drifted back to finding Jen on her cabin floor, eyes squeezed shut, Bible clutched to her heart, thanking God for sending him. He tried to swallow past the lump swelling in his throat. She hadn't known he was standing there. He was sure of it. He only wished his motives were as pure as she believed. If he'd doubted her innocence and faith before, he didn't now. He glanced at her profile, her blond hair cascading over her shoulders, and prayed she wouldn't hate him when he came clean.

Jen soon joined him at his computer. "My internet connection dropped. But not one that I checked was reported stolen. Maybe Cass was right and the painting I saw was just a reproduction."

"Was it on the list?"

Jen ran her finger down the rest of the column. "No."

Sam showed her the page she'd given him. "Not on mine, either."

"And if it was a legitimate purchase, it should be." Jen frowned at the marked out list of names. "You didn't expect any of these to be on the FBI's list, did you?"

He shrugged. His cohort had taken photocopies to cross-check; he just hadn't reported his findings back to Sam.

"So we really don't know if there have been any others beside the painting I found."

No, and it was looking less and less like Jen could supply them with any evidence. "Not unless you can find them in storage or a paper trail of their purchase or sale." Sam reached for the mouse. "Let's find your sister." The best they could hope for was that Blake was right about his father being on a buying trip and they could set a trap for him when he returned.

"Wait one second. Before you log off, can you check the Seattle news outlets to see if that reporter's fishing expedition has reached home?"

Sam visited the main sites for Seattle news, then did a general search across the web. "Not a peep."

Jen blew out a breath. "That's a relief. Maybe if I can convince Cass to agree, we'll be able to quietly sell after all—after turning in the stolen painting, of course."

"Maybe." His attention caught by a photo on the screen, Sam scarcely registered Jen's words. "Oh, wow."

"What is it?" Jen's hair brushed his cheek as she peered over his shoulder.

He drew a deep breath, enjoying the flowery scent that was uniquely hers.

"Sherri Steele," Jen read from the caption under the photo of a paramedic cradling a newborn. "Is she related?"

"Yeah, a cousin."

"Says she saved the baby's life. He wasn't breathing when he was born."

Sam's throat thickened. "Yeah, that smile says it all." He hadn't seen Sherri since Jake's wedding six years ago. She'd still been a spindly teen, all legs and arms.

"We have to tell your parents! A hero in your very own family. Although I guess with Jake being a firefighter, he's probably saved a few lives too, right?"

"Yeah." Sam swallowed but not soon enough to clear the emotion from his throat. He clicked off the computer and hoped Jen hadn't noticed.

The sparkle in her eyes dimmed. "You remembering Jimmy?"

He pressed his lips together and blinked hard to escape the last of the memory. "Yeah."

She tugged him to his feet and steered him toward an upholstered loveseat tucked against a wide window and away from passersby. Taking a seat, she pulled him down beside her. "Tell me about him."

Something akin to panic seized his chest. "Jimmy?"

"Yes. Reminiscing helps. Trust me."

The sincerity in her pure blue eyes slowed his rampaging pulse. Her eyes reminded him of the kind of skies they'd always prayed for as kids on family gathering days.

She didn't say anything more, just waited.

An image of Jimmy rose to his mind and a smile found its way to his lips. "He was a cute kid. Always giggling. A chatterbox."

Jen squeezed his hand. "Losing him must have left a big hole in your family."

"Yeah. Jake and two of my other cousins became firefighters. Sherri became a paramedic. I think they wanted to redeem Jimmy's death by trying to spare other families from the loss we faced."

"Wow, that's pretty noble."

"Yeah." He hoped she couldn't hear the self-loathing that bled through the single word.

"You never told me how you ended up in Boston."

Oh, yeah, she'd heard it. He exhaled, wishing he hadn't let her scrape open old wounds. He'd been handling the scars just fine.

"Sam?" She tilted her head until he met her gaze.

"It was about as far away from Seattle as I could get without crossing an ocean."

"Because seeing your family with Jimmy missing was too hard."

He blinked, surprised by how close to the truth she'd guessed.

She offered him a bittersweet smile. "Sounds like we both handle grief the same way."

Grasping at the opportunity to shift the focus away from him, he squeezed her hand. "You're thinking about your parents?"

"Yeah. They were driving home from a gala. The roads were slick. The police said they took the curve too fast for the conditions. For years after their deaths, I refused to go to the gallery or anything connected to it."

"And you're still trying to get away."

She shrugged. "Just like you."

"Touché." Except no one at the gallery blamed her for her parents' death.

"How'd the fire start?"

Sam pulled away. He couldn't do this. They needed to find Cass. He had an investigation to finish.

"I'm sorry." Jen reached for his hand, those watery blue eyes reeling him in. "I didn't mean to pry. It's just…I care about you."

His heart squeezed, self-recrimination swamping the delight he wanted to feel at her words. He cupped her hand between his. "I'm okay."

"No, you're not," she said, clearly not planning to drop the subject. And strangely, her determination made him want to tell her about it, given how much else there was that he couldn't.

"Okay, I found my cousin messing with my girl. Only, I didn't know that while I was away at college, she'd become *his* girl, so I laid into him. He dropped his cigarette to fight back."

"And the barn caught fire." Her voice filled with undeserved sympathy.

"Yeah." His heart felt like a hundred-pound weight in his chest. Jen must've heard it in his voice.

"It was an accident," she said softly. "I'm sure your family doesn't blame you."

Tumbling into her compassionate gaze, he could almost believe it was true. More than that, she filled him with yearnings he hadn't entertained since the day Jimmy died. Like living close to family, having kids, getting together so the cousins could play.

He shook his head. She didn't even know he was an agent. And as much as he wanted to tell her, he couldn't risk it. Continuing to play the friend while helping her feed information to the police was smarter.

He looked up and spotted Cass behind a computer at the internet café. "Hey, I found your sister. C'mon."

Intent on the computer screen in front of her, Cass didn't seem to notice their approach, and her ear-to-ear smile sparked suspicions Sam hated to entertain. He needed to get his eyes on the screen before she spotted them and shut it down. He tugged Jen sideways to veer around behind Cass.

"What are you doing?" Jen jerked against his hold.

He pulled out his cell phone and activated the camera. "Trust me."

Jen gasped as he snapped photos of her sister's computer screen.

Cass spun her chair at the sound. "Jen! Great news, I found Uncle Reggie." She shimmied her chair sideways, giving Jen full view of the screen.

"He emailed you?"

Sam scrutinized the sender's email address and surreptitiously texted the Seattle office, asking them to trace the IP address. Anyone could have sent the email, but the IP address would at least tell them where it came from.

"He has a seller in Ketchikan he wants us to meet," Cass explained, scrolling the screen up.

"That's it?" Jen squinted at the message. "Didn't he say where he is? Why he closed the gallery?"

"No." Cass pulled the keyboard toward her. "I'll ask."

Sam tugged back her chair. "Wait." This had setup written all over it. "What have you already told him?"

"I told him Jen wanted out…." Her voice turned sheepish as she met Jen's horrified expression. "I asked if he'd want to buy your share."

Jen sank into the chair beside Cass. "Please tell me you didn't tell him about my suspicions."

"Of course not!"

Sam rested his palm on Jen's trembling shoulder and scrutinized the nuances of Cass's expression—the eye dilation, the red cheeks, the indignation in her tone.

"He hasn't gone into hiding like you thought. The gallery in Skagway didn't give us a stolen painting like you thought. You can't still believe that he's doing anything illegal?" She jerked her computer mouse to the log out button. "You always had a wild imagination." She rose as if the conversation was over.

"I don't think it's her imagination," Sam countered with a tone that pinned Cass back into her chair.

She tilted her head and studied him. "You really think Reg is moving stolen paintings through the gallery?"

"I want to."

"Want to?" She looked at him as if he had two heads.

"It beats the alternative."

"Which is?"

He glanced at the passengers on the other computer terminals and lowered his voice. "That someone *else* at the gallery is."

She planted her hands on her hips. "I'm the only other one there."

"Exactly," Jen said, as if that should settle the argument. "And if we don't sell soon, you could get caught up in the consequences. The police aren't going to believe you didn't know about the stolen painting."

"I don't believe this. Now you're using Sam to try to blackmail me into agreeing to sell."

"Cass, it's not like that."

"Look, if you want out, I get that. I'm sure Uncle Reggie will figure out a way to make it work."

Sam exhaled. That's what he was afraid of.

THIRTEEN

"Yes, I want *out* of the gallery," Jen said low enough so the passengers at neighboring computers wouldn't hear. "But not by getting pushed into a glacial river. And for the record, Cass, *that* wasn't a figment of my imagination." Buoyed by Sam's supportive shoulder squeeze, she produced the unsigned card they'd found in the cabin. "Who sent this?"

Cass's face flamed. Her gaze flicked to Sam. "Where'd you find that?"

Jen tensed at Cass's avoidance of the question. "Does it matter?"

"Can we please talk about this later?" Cass asked through gritted teeth.

"Why are you being so secretive?"

Cass glared. "Because I like Jake and—" she motioned toward Sam with a subtle tilt of her head and lowered her voice "—I don't want his brother telling him I'm seeing someone else."

"Are you?"

Cass rolled her eyes. "You know me. The card was from Blake. He slipped it into the front of the novel he gave me for the trip. He promised me a night on the town to celebrate turning twenty-five."

Jen shifted uneasily. It sounded like something he'd do. Had she gotten all weirded out over nothing?

"Let's just forget about it. Okay?" Cass flipped her hair off her shoulder and tootled her fingers to someone behind them.

"Here you are." Jake joined them with Tommy in tow. "I thought we might have a Ping-Pong match. They say it'll be another couple of hours before the ship reaches the glaciers."

"I'm game," Cass gushed and turned to Jen. "When you and Sam went out to take the phone call last night, the magician did a trick with a Ping-Pong ball and I mentioned to Jake that we used to be pretty good Ping-Pong players."

Despite her irritation with her sister, Jen couldn't help but laugh at the glint in her eye. Super competitive didn't come close to describing Cass at any game. "Did you happen to mention we were college champs?"

Sam elbowed his brother. "That sounds like a challenge."

Two games later, with Tommy and his grandparents cheering from the sidelines, Cass sliced the Ping-Pong ball across the table, straight into Sam's chest. "Oops, sor-ry."

"No, you're not! You *could* take a *little* sympathy on us, you know." His gaze strayed to a point behind them, and his grin slipped.

Jen glanced over her shoulder but couldn't see what

had disturbed him. Their gazes met across the table, and her stomach dipped at the definite change in his mood.

"Speak for yourself," Jake piped up. "I want to win this game fair and square."

"Win?" Sam looked at his brother like he'd just boarded the wrong ship. "They've already skunked us two games straight. I'd be happy to just score a point."

Cass laughed. "What do you think, Jen? Should we give them an easy one?"

Jen searched Sam's eyes, confused by how easily he'd slipped back into the role of teasing opponent. "Sure, why not?"

Schooling her expression into the picture of kind-heartedness, Cass lobbed a deceptively gentle ball to Sam's corner of the table.

As he drew back his paddle, the spin she'd put on the ball sent it bouncing the opposite way and he swiped air. Kind of like the spin Cass seemed to be putting on everything connected to the gallery and the attacks.

The Steeles laughed at Sam's miss.

He tossed his paddle onto the table. "Okay, I concede. You win."

Jen rounded the table to offer him a good-game handshake. "I'm sorry. That last lob was mean."

Sam edged his cell phone from his pocket and frowned at the screen before clasping her hand. "Just the last one, huh?" Amusement rippled through his voice. He tugged her close. "After that whooping, I should at least get a hug, don't you think?"

She wrapped her arms around his waist as his parents smiled on.

Happiness bubbled in her chest. She couldn't remember when she'd had more fun. If only Cass would see how enjoyable life could be apart from the glamour and glitz of gallery parties. This was what Jen had always dreamed of having—family, the center of her world, people who loved her for herself, like it used to be before Mom and Dad bought the gallery.

"I'll take losing any time if it wins me a hug like this." Sam gave her an extra-warm squeeze and whispered close to her ear, "We need to talk."

Blindsided by his ominous tone, she tried to step back, but Sam didn't loosen his hold. When she lifted her gaze, his lips hovered inches from hers.

She went still—very still.

Jake cleared his throat and Sam immediately shifted to her side, catching her by the elbow. "We'll see you guys later."

"What?" Jen's gaze bounced from her sister to Jake to Sam to his parents as she frantically tried to figure out what was going on.

Cass waved her off. "Go."

Sam steered her toward the stairs that led to the half deck overlooking the pool and Ping-Pong tables. "Where'd you and your sister learn to play like that?"

Jen glanced back at his family and Cass. "Sam, what's going on?"

"I'll explain when I'm certain we won't be overheard." His hold on her arm tightened as he picked up his pace. "Where'd you learn to play like that?"

Her pulse galloped. He expected her to have a casual conversation as if he wasn't whisking her away like some undercover cop in a movie?

He veered left at the top of the stairs. "Jen?"

"Our dad was crazy about Ping-Pong. Cass and I played so much as kids that we could anticipate each other's moves. It made us good partners."

"I've heard twins can practically read each other's minds. That true?"

"Sam, why are you asking me these questions?"

He stopped and turned her toward the rail. Resting his forearms on it, he casually let his gaze travel over the deck below. "See the red-haired woman in the yellow top by the bar?"

"Yeah."

"She was watching us play."

"So? We kept you guys hopping. I'm sure lots of people were watching."

Sam rhythmically brushed his thumb over his fisted fingers. "She's Bellamy's roommate."

"What?" Jen tracked the woman's gaze toward where Cass and Jake had joined his parents and Tommy in lounge chairs. Her stomach tumbled. "But the detective said she didn't seem to know what Bellamy had been up to. Do you think she'll try to hurt one of us?"

"She didn't watch you leave the deck," Sam said, as if that should make her feel better. "So I need to know… How well can you read your sister?"

"I don't understand what you mean." Did Sam think the woman was trying to make contact with

Cass? He must. Why else would he ask how well she could read Cass? Her heart raced like a runaway train. A train that had jumped the tracks and careened off a cliff, one car plowing into the next.

Sam laced his fingers through hers. "I mean, do you think Cass could be lying about what she knows about your uncle's dealings?"

"I don't know what to think!"

"So you concede that her protests could just be an act to throw you off her trail?"

Jen's throat closed at hearing him voice her secret fear. She shook her head as much to convince herself as Sam.

"I know you don't want to believe it, Jen. But you admitted that you rarely visited the gallery."

"I might have avoided the gallery. But I *know* my sister."

"Are you sure? Cass's protests that your guardian would never sell stolen art might sound so believable because they're true."

Jen swallowed past the clog in her throat. She didn't want to lose her sister, but Lord help her, she suspected her, too.

Sam squeezed her hand. "I'm sorry, Jen. I know this can't be easy for you."

The breeze off the icy water shivered over her as she glanced at the red-haired woman and then her sister.

"Had you mentioned your desire to sell to Cass before that incident outside the restaurant in Seattle?"

Drawing a deep breath, Jen tipped back her head

and revisited the day in her mind. The cloud-packed sky had looked as gloomy as she'd felt. "No, I didn't. Why?"

"I'm trying to figure out who knew what when the attacks started."

"Cass was with me. She couldn't have wrecked my car."

"But she could've kept you occupied and reported where you were parked to a partner."

Jen shook her head. "Next you'll be saying she faked being sick so she could sic someone after me on that white-water rafting excursion."

The slight widening of Sam's eyes, as if he seriously expected her to consider the possibility, made her heart jolt. "No, I won't believe it. Cass would never hurt me." But even as the words left her mouth, doubts niggled. "Okay, I admit that I didn't like the sound of meeting some stranger in Ketchikan on Uncle Reggie's say-so, especially after Cass told him I want to sell my share in the gallery."

"Which is why you can't put off admitting your suspicions to the police any longer. Bellamy may be warming a prison cell in Juneau, but that woman down there could be plotting to finish his mission. And if the investigation into Bellamy exposes dealings with your uncle, as I suspect, or with your sister, and they learn you've withheld information, you could be charged with obstruction of justice."

The blood drained from her face. Jen locked her knees and gripped the rail as blackness clouded her vision. All she'd wanted was out.

Sam showed her a text message he'd received. "I forwarded Detective Reed the information in the email Cass got. It was sent from an IP address in Juneau."

Jen's hand flew to her throat. "Reggie's in Alaska?"

Sam collected new tour tickets at the shore excursion desk. Once again they'd forfeited the cost of their prepaid tours, this time for Ketchikan, but better that than being caught in a trap. He pocketed the tickets and headed back to their deck.

Hopefully the others wouldn't be too disappointed about missing out on geocaching, but the idea of their treasure hunting in a rainforest on a remote island, where Reggie or another of his minions could be lying in wait, didn't sit well with him. Tommy would be disappointed, but perhaps riding a San Francisco–style trolley car and seeing the world's largest totem pole collection would make up for it.

Rounding the stairs to the next deck, Sam glanced at the painting decorating the landing. Since Jennifer had given the go-ahead yesterday afternoon for the Seattle FBI to secretly search the gallery for stolen paintings, incriminating paperwork or anything that might help them locate Reggie, she'd been more edgy than ever.

He'd yet to tell her that they'd found nada. Or that their interrogation of her buyer yielded nothing more than unsubstantiated rumors. Not that it meant Reggie was innocent. Far from it. If he'd clued in that Jen was on to him, he'd probably gone out of his way to destroy everything that might link him to anything illegal. But the lack of evidence, not to mention Jennifer's waning confidence that the painting she'd purportedly seen was an original, didn't bode well for his case.

The likelihood of recovering an important and valuable Native American painting had been the key to convincing his boss to let him take the case. Now that its recovery wasn't in the picture and Jen had arguably given them all the help she could, Sam had had to do some quick talking to convince his boss not to cut the trip short and recall him to Boston.

Thankfully his boss had agreed that Michaels's sudden disappearance after the botched attempt on Jennifer's life was highly suspicious. His apparent reappearance in Juneau was more so. Could be he'd come to ensure Bellamy's silence. Could be he'd come to pick up the stolen painting himself. Could be he wasn't there at all and an imposter had sent Cass the email to manipulate them into a meeting.

"There you are," Cass said from the doorway of her cabin as he turned down the hall. "I was ready to propose a shopping trip if you didn't show up soon."

"Everyone ready?" Sam produced the tickets from his shirt pocket as Jen and his family crowded in behind Cass. "City highlights by trolley, including a tour of a totem pole park, and you'll still have plenty of time left for shopping."

Cass snorted her lack of enthusiasm. "I don't understand why we can't go geocaching, since Bellamy's still in jail."

Sam herded them toward the elevator. "Better safe than sorry." A fistful of unknowns on an undercover case was nothing new to him. He never took anything for granted. Thinking an indictment was in the bag was what got agents killed. In this case, it could get Jennifer killed. So until the agents in Juneau located Reggie, he wasn't taking any chances.

Buses and vans, awaiting tour participants, lined the street adjoining the pier. Sam ensured his entourage bypassed the minibus that would have delivered them to the launch site for the geocaching tour in case someone was watching for them. His FBI contact in Juneau had alerted the local Ketchikan police to be on the lookout for Reggie, but with thousands of new faces pouring off cruise ships every day, Sam didn't expect anything to come of the effort—if Reggie was even in the town.

"What is it?" The nervousness in Jen's voice said she'd noticed him eyeballing the crowds, and he hadn't missed the way her hand tightened on his arm every time a redhead jostled past them.

Bellamy's roommate had spent last night in the casino and wasn't booked on any of the ship-arranged tours, but his FBI contact had arranged for an alert to be texted to Sam's cell phone if she swiped her card to leave the ship.

Jen's pace slowed, causing them to fall behind the others. "Have you heard from the police about the gallery search?"

Cass glanced back at them before he could respond.

"See that jewelry store? I want to go there when we get back."

"Ooh," Sam's mom gushed. "Good plan."

Jen's smile looked forced, but he wasn't sure if it was sparked by the idea of jewelry shopping or having her question interrupted. He traced his thumb down her bare fingers. He'd never been jewelry shopping, but he had a strong urge to change that.

Cass gushed on about a gemstone she'd learned about through one of the ship's shopping spotlights as Jen groaned under her breath.

"We'll talk later," Sam whispered, pretty sure that not getting an answer to her question was what had soured her mood. Then again, Cass had confided in Jake that Jen had been engaged once, so maybe...

Unlike on their White Pass bus tour, Cass urged Jen to share a seat with Sam, and Cass and Jake squeezed Tommy onto one with them. She was actually starting to be pretty good with the kid, much better than the day they'd boarded.

As the trolley pulled out of the lot past the line of buses, Cass's head snapped from the window beside her to the one at the back of the bus. "Stop the bus," she shouted and tugged on the bell rope strung above the windows.

The bus driver braked and glanced in his rearview mirror. "What's going on?"

"I think I saw Reggie." Cass climbed over Jake's knees. "We have to get off. C'mon, Jen."

Jen shot Sam a panicked look.

Adrenaline surging, he twisted in his seat to see

if he could confirm Cass's sighting because he had a bad feeling it was a ploy to lure Jen into danger.

"I can't wait for you," the bus driver declared. "You'll miss the tour."

Cass was already halfway up the aisle while the rest of his family and Jen seemed to be looking to him to make the call. Did he dare let Cass leave on her own? Would she?

The other passengers grew louder, demanding they hurry up and decide.

Cass stopped three seats from the front and looked back at them. "Jen? Aren't you coming? He was standing outside the bus we were supposed to be at. Probably came to surprise us for our birthday."

Jen's face drained of color. Thinking that might not be the only surprise he, *or Cass,* had in mind.

The driver opened the front door of the bus. "I'm blocking traffic here. Are you getting off or not?"

"Cass, we can't," Jen pleaded. "It was probably just someone who looks like him. I don't want to miss the tour."

Sam suspected that either way she wasn't going to enjoy it, and if Cass wasn't lying, he hated to give up the opportunity to confront the man. The bus Jen and Cass were meant to be on pulled onto the road ahead of the trolley. No one remained at the bus stop.

Cass peered out the side window and threw up her hands. "We've missed him."

The driver closed the door. "So you're staying?"

"I guess." Cass trudged back to her seat as Sam discreetly texted the possible sighting to the local PD.

Cass glanced at his phone. "Your phone works here?" She flopped back into her seat and pulled out her own.

Sam caught Jake's attention and silently urged him to monitor the call.

She thumbed in a text message then held the phone up to the window. "I lost the signal."

The trolley car rounded a corner, climbing higher up the mountainous town that had more "streets" built as stairs than paved roads. As Cass shifted the phone to a myriad of positions, Jake squinted at the screen.

"There!" Cass shouted as the message apparently went out.

"You texted Reg?" Jen asked.

"Yeah, told him I thought I saw him and asked if he's in Ketchikan to surprise us."

In front of Cass, Sam's dad turned in his seat. "Did you tell him where we were going?"

"Yeah, the totem pole park, right?"

Dad met Sam's gaze, obviously cluing in to the potentially dangerous consequences of Cass's blunder…if it was a blunder.

They'd have to be extra vigilant from the moment they stepped off the trolley.

Cass's phone vibrated. "Oh, he got it!" She pulled up the message. "Yeah, he says he guesses the surprise was on him. He wants us to get off at Creek Street at the end of the tour and he'll meet us there for a late lunch."

Creek Street was a re-creation of the city's old "red-light district." And red lights—screaming setup—were flashing in Sam's head. The question was how many men could the local police mobilize in less than ninety minutes to help patrol the area? And did he really want to rally them? His boss would ship him to Nome if he was wrong.

Sam texted the request anyway and asked his FBI contact to try again to get a GPS fix on Reggie's cell phone. He hated going into an area blind, and although he'd studied the map of downtown Ketchikan, he'd never walked it. He didn't know what blind alley someone could be hiding on.

He glanced across the aisle at Jake and Cass. They seemed absorbed by the trolley driver's colorful tales, so Sam showed Jen the picture on his cell phone he'd snapped of Cass's computer screen, zooming in on the list of recent emails. "You know any of these guys?" Three other names besides Reggie's had sent her email messages since the start of the cruise.

"I think Doug is a guy Cass sometimes dates. You know about Blake. And—" Jen let out a choked gasp, confirming this was the Ian he thought it was.

Not that he intended to let on that he knew about her canceled engagement. "Who's Ian?" he asked, hoping her trust had deepened enough to tell him.

Jen shook her head. "I don't know."

Sam cocked his head, eyebrow raised. "Try again."

Pulling the screen closer, Jen squinted at the listing. "I know *an* Ian, but I can't see the email address to know if it's him."

Sam zoomed in. "Ian number one at date me dot com."

Jen glared in her sister's direction. "I can't believe she'd give him the time of day, let alone her email address!"

"Shh." Sam gently caught Jen's chin so she'd refocus on him. The last thing he wanted was Cass knowing how deep his suspicions ran. "Who is he?"

"Nobody important."

"Jen, I'm trying to keep you safe. If this guy's been corresponding with your sister, we need to know why."

She pulled away and turned toward the window. "My ex-fiancé. Is that enough information for you?"

Not by a long shot. His heart did a rolling dive at the depth of her bitterness. "Why'd you break up?"

"Because he was just using me to get what he wanted."

Sam swallowed at how uncomfortably close that sounded to how she might describe him if he ever came clean. Not that coming clean had ever been in the game plan. But neither had falling for his suspect.

"Apparently Cass didn't learn from my experience," Jen said so quietly he almost didn't hear her.

He cradled her hand between his. "I'm sorry."

"Don't be. I'm just glad I found out before it was too late."

"What was it, exactly, he'd wanted?"

"The prestige, connections and wealth he seemed to think marrying me would bring."

"Is there any way he might benefit from your death?"

Her attention jerked back to him. "No!"

"Unless he married your sister."

FOURTEEN

As the trolley pulled away, Jen scanned the shops along the boardwalk on the opposite side of the creek. "I don't see Reggie." But her gaze skittered over more than one man who seemed to be watching them.

She tightened her grip on her purse and stepped closer to Sam. It wasn't unusual for people to stare at her and Cass. People seemed to have a fascination with identical twins. But under the circumstances, being stared at felt downright creepy.

Even though the Steeles wouldn't know what their uncle looked like, Sam and his brother and father all scanned the area, too. Jake mumbled something to Sam, pointing to the same men Jen had noticed, but Sam didn't appear concerned. One of the men even nodded at him. With his experience in security, Sam could probably tell a shady character when he saw one.

Her heart settled back into a normal rhythm knowing they were watching out for trouble.

Cass did a three-sixty scan of the area, then pulled

out her phone. "I'll text him to let him know where we are."

A second after Cass hit Send, an old-fashioned ringtone sounded from the direction of the board-walk, and Sam's attention snapped that way.

"It must be a coincidence," Jen whispered when the man with the phone turned and lifted it to his ear...not how anyone would answer a text message.

Sam's gaze narrowed as the guy slipped inside the shop. "You recognize him?"

Jen frowned. "No, why?"

"Just checking."

Cass's phone rang. "I got a message back. Reg says he's sorry. He got tied up and can't get away just yet. He suggests we do some shopping and he'll text as soon as he's free."

Jen shot Sam a "what now?" glance. Should she be concerned? She'd scarcely heard a word the tour guide said at the totem pole park for worrying about what Uncle Reggie would say. Deep down she still couldn't believe he'd come all this way to hurt her, but she had a bad feeling he had come to talk her out of selling the gallery. And considering how many years he'd devoted to keeping it for them, she hated how ungrateful she must look for having tried to orches-trate the sale behind his back. But she'd known he wouldn't approve, and she didn't want to fight him. Not then and not now.

"Why don't we visit that jewelry store?" Sam's mom suggested cheerily.

"Can I borrow your phone first?" Sam asked Cass.

She gave him a funny look but obliged. Sam scrolled through her screens and seemed to find what he was looking for, which Jen was more curious about than ever. He pushed a button then brought the phone to his ear.

Jen could hear the muffled sound of the ringtone, and after the second one, noticed a faint echo of it drifting across the creek. She scanned the crowds along with Sam as the third ring sounded.

He glanced at the phone and handed it back to Cass.

"What is it?" Jen asked.

"The phone cut out."

"Yeah," Cass said. "The reception around here isn't that great."

Sam cupped Jen's elbow. "We should go back to the ship."

Cass stomped her foot. "Who died and put you in charge? This is our last chance to souvenir shop, and I want to check out the jewelry store."

Sam's dad clapped Sam's shoulder. "She's right, son."

Some unspoken communication seemed to happen between Sam and his dad, and Sam reluctantly nodded.

Sam's mom and dad led the way to the jewelry store, and as Sam fell back, checking his own phone, Cass hooked her arm through Jen's and urged her ahead. "Since when do you let any guy call the shots?"

"Since someone drugged me and pushed me in a glacial river and—"

"Are you sure he's the good guy? I mean, he's been at every scene."

Jen's heart hiccupped.

"Why's he so interested?" Cass hissed close to Jen's ear, slanting a glance back at Jake and Sam and Tommy. "He's even got the cops calling him with updates. What's with that?"

"He's in security," Jen argued, trying to ignore a sudden niggling doubt. "He knows how these investigations work. He wants to keep us safe." She couldn't be wrong about him, not when he'd jumped into an icy river to rescue her.

"Seems more like he's trying to turn you against me."

Jen bumped shoulders with her. "Will never happen." The episode at the computer yesterday flashed through Jen's mind, pinching her chest. She'd sided with Sam then, too. She wanted to keep Cass safe and close, but…she couldn't ignore her suspicions.

Sam's mom stopped in front of a different jewelry store than the one Cass had pointed out earlier. "Shall we check this one out?"

"Sure." Cass released Jen's arm and followed Mrs. Steele in.

Jake elbowed his dad. "I hope you hid Mom's credit card before letting her loose in there."

Mr. Steele chuckled. "She deserves something nice for putting up with me for forty years."

"I hope you know what you're doing…." Jake let his voice trail off as his father held open the door for them. Jake hoisted Tommy in his arms. "No touching in the store. Okay?" He nodded to a display of crystal ornaments. "Because if you break it, we buy it, and...your daddy can't afford it."

With everyone else busy gawking at jewelry, Jen took the opportunity to pull Sam aside. "What happened back there? Who did you call?"

"I dialed your uncle's number. Whoever answered immediately hung up."

Jen's heart started an erratic war dance in her chest. "But maybe Cass was right and the reception cut out."

"You heard the phone ring. Whoever was on the other end was watching us, and my guess is he didn't answer because he didn't want us to pick him out of the crowd."

The dance in her chest quickened. "What do you mean, whoever? I thought you called Uncle Reggie."

"I did, but then why didn't he answer when Cass's number appeared on his screen?"

"Because he 'saw' it was you, not Cassie calling."

"Yeah, or because it wasn't really him on the other end and whoever it was didn't want Cass to know."

Jen opened her mouth to protest, but Sam raised his hand.

"Think about it. All communication before that was by text. Why didn't he just call?"

Nibbling on her fingernail, Jen watched Cass try on rings. She didn't know what to think anymore.

Sam rested his arm at the small of her back and urged her deeper into the store. "I'm sorry. I didn't mean to spoil your last day in Alaska with worrying. I just want you, and Cass, to be safe."

Jen could only nod and silently thank God once again for sending Sam to help them.

Sam stopped in front of a display case of diamond rings his mother was admiring.

"Which style do you prefer?" Mrs. Steele asked Jen.

"Me? Oh." Jen strolled along the display case, studying the rows of diamonds. Seeing one similar to her ring from Ian, she cringed at the memory of the grotesquely large solitaire ring he'd presented her when he proposed. "Nothing too large." She moved on to a display of other gemstone rings. "I like these with a colorful gemstone in the middle, set off on either side by a few small diamonds."

Sam stepped beside her, the warmth of his presence chasing away the chilly memory of Ian's proposal but not before she remembered his recent email to Cass.

She'd have to get her sister alone to ask about what she was doing emailing Ian. Not that Jen thought for a second Cass would ever consider marrying the jerk.

Sam's breath tickled her ear. "Which gemstone is *your* favorite?"

What? Her heart kicked. Not that she thought for a second that Sam had more than a casual interest. Reminders of Ian had just— Ian was the last person she should give the satisfaction of spoiling her day. She shoved him from her mind and focused on the rings. "That one." She pointed to a stone that seemed to radiate a rainbow of colors.

"Can we go to a toy store?" Tommy whined.

Cass laughed. "How about we find you a genuine Indian war bonnet? Or maybe a Davy Crockett raccoon-tail cap?"

"Yeah!" Tommy looked at Cass with unabashed adoration, drawing a chuckle from Jake.

"And you were telling *me* to guard my credit card," Mr. Steele teased.

Jen pressed a hand to her heart at the family interplay, recalling a long-ago similar remark by her dad.

"You okay?" Sam grazed a finger down her arm.

"Oh." She caught herself twisting her necklace and self-consciously lowered her arm. "Just tired, I guess."

"Did you want to return to the ship? Have a rest?"

Jen looked to Cass, who shrugged. "You do what you want. Tommy and I are going to find a coon hat. Aren't we, bud?"

"Yeah!" Tommy squealed, clutching Cass's hand.

Jen smiled at how good Cass had become with him. "You have fun. Call me when you hear from Uncle Reggie."

Sam leaned close to his dad and whispered something. A few minutes later, Jen headed back to the ship with Sam, reassured that Jake and Mr. Steele would keep her sister out of danger.

"We could lie on deck in a couple of lounge chairs for a bit, enjoy the sunshine. What do you think?" Sam asked.

"Sounds great. I wouldn't mind grabbing my book from the cabin first, though."

They took their time returning to the ship, window shopping along the way. Jen suspected from Sam's surreptitious glance over his shoulder every other minute that he was on the lookout for Reg or someone else equally dangerous.

Spotting a little Inuit doll in a store window, Sam popped inside and bought it. "My boss's wife just had a baby girl," he explained.

Jen marveled at how sweet he was. Not many guys would think to get a gift, let alone something so uniquely special. Forty-five minutes later they finally reached their cabins.

"You have a message." Sam pointed to the envelope in the holder outside her door.

Jen opened it and blinked a few times to make sure she was reading it right.

"What is it?" Sam asked.

"A note from Reg asking us to meet him on the pier when we get back. He says he lost his cell phone. He bought a new one but couldn't remember our phone numbers. He says he has something important to discuss."

Their steward came out of a nearby room.

"Excuse me," Sam called out. "Do you happen to know when this message came in for Miss Robbins?"

"Yes, a crew member delivered it this morning, said someone brought it to the ship."

"Thank you." Sam took Jen's key and opened her cabin. "I don't know what to think. I thought maybe whoever I tried to call on the cell phone might've planted the note as another way to lure you to them."

"But this really is Uncle Reggie's handwriting. It's very distinctive. See the extra flourishes he puts on his letters?"

"Maybe this was his backup plan if his Creek Street plan didn't work."

Jen shuddered. "You mean his supposed plan to hurt us?"

Sam looked apologetic. "Yes."

"But that doesn't make any sense. If we were hurt at Creek Street, the police would've checked Cass's phone and known she was meeting Reg. If he went to all the trouble to stage attacks a thousand miles away from where he is, why would he incriminate himself?"

"Don't you see? That's the beauty of leaving the note claiming he'd lost his phone. Because he only ever texted Cass, she can't know for sure that the texts were from your uncle. It would explain why he didn't answer when I called."

Jen shuddered. "So what do we do? Meet him? We can't exactly sic the police on him. We have no proof he's behind anything."

Sam pulled out his phone. "Jake, where are you now?" Sam listened. "Good, we'll meet you on the pier." Sam grabbed Jen's hand. "Let's go."

Not even the confidence in his tone and firm grasp could make her muscles move. "What? You just finished saying Reg was trying to lure me into danger and now you want to walk straight into it?"

He prodded her forward. "Don't worry. I have no intention of letting him get too close to you." He stopped her halfway down the gangplank. "Do you see him anywhere?"

"No."

Jake flagged Sam, then headed to a shop at the end of the pier.

Sam steered Jen toward Cass and Tommy, who wore a Davy Crockett hat. They were standing hand in hand at the pier's edge, peering into the water. "Let's catch up with your sister."

"Hey, guys." Cass hitched her thumb toward a shop. "Jake's getting us ice cream. Want some?"

"No, thanks. Cass…" Jen drew Uncle Reggie's note from her pocket.

"Oh, look." Cass pointed to the open water. "A pod of whales!"

Her exclamation drew an immediate crowd.

Sam touched Jen's arm. "I'm going to make a quick call." His gaze scanned the crowd even as he spoke.

Tommy tugged at Cassie's shirt. "I can't see."

To Jen's astonishment, Cass scooped Tommy into her arms and pointed again. "See?"

The crowd closed in on them, their gazes tracking the direction Cass pointed. Clutching the note, Jen edged out of the way of clicking cameras. Suddenly, Cass screamed.

Shouts rose. A loud splash.

"Cass!" Heart pounding, Jen pushed through the crowd just as Cass disappeared under the water, clutching Tommy. "Sam!" Jen frantically searched the dark water. *Please, Lord.*

Cass bobbed to the surface, a sputtering Tommy still in her arms. She pushed him toward Jen. "Take him."

"I've got him." Sam moved her out of the way and lifted Tommy free of the icy water. The haunted expression on Sam's face as he clutched his shivering nephew to his chest punched the air from her lungs.

"My hat," Tommy wailed as Sam wrapped him in his coat.

Cass dove back under and emerged a few seconds later, lifting the hat in victory. "Got it, Tommy!" In three strong strokes, she was at the ladder, and Jen offered her a hand out. Cassie's lips were already blue. Jen peeled off her own jacket and dropped it over Cassie's shoulders. "You did good, sis."

"Out of my way." Jake's voice sounded over the milling crowd. As the people stepped aside, the ice cream cones dropped from Jake's hands. He ripped Tommy from Sam's arms. "This has gone too far. You've endangered my son!"

Sam swallowed the apology burning his throat, hoping the twins wouldn't question what Jake's accusation meant. When he'd heard the splash, seen Tommy flailing, seen his head dip beneath the water, it'd been the fire and cousin Jimmy all over again. Jake could take a strip out of his hide, but nothing could make Sam feel any worse than seeing the terror in his nephew's eyes.

"It was an accident," Jen said, except the crack in her voice betrayed how responsible she felt.

Not that Jake was listening as he frantically checked every inch of his drenched son between clutching him to his chest.

Now that Tommy had his raccoon hat back, he looked thrilled to be the center of attention. "Auntie Cass saved my hat," he declared, and the crowd chuckled at the understatement.

"I'm sorry, Jake," Cass said. "I picked him up to give him a better view of the whales, and the crowd pressed in so close behind us, we got knocked in."

Sam scanned the dispersing crowd for Reginald Michaels. No way was this an accident. Michaels must have seen his opportunity to finish Jen off, except that from behind, Jen and Cass looked identical, and he probably hadn't imagined in a million years that Cass would be the one of the pair holding a child.

Jake gave her a one-armed hug. "It's not your fault. Thank you for saving him."

"And my hat," Tommy blurted.

Jake's lips inched into a half smile. "And his hat."

A cool breeze swept in off the water, making Tommy's teeth chatter.

Jen urged them toward the gangplank. "We'd better get him aboard and into dry clothes."

Now that Tommy was safe, Sam hesitated, hating to miss the chance to catch Michaels.

Jen must've mistaken his hesitation for guilt. "I'm so sorry."

Sam fell into step beside her as seagulls scavenging for dropped morsels squawked out of their way. "For what?"

"For causing animosity between you and your brother. I know this was an accident, but he's right. We never should have involved you in our troubles and put Tommy at risk."

Sam swallowed a relieved sigh at her assumption. The last thing he felt like doing right now—ever—was explaining what Jake had really meant.

Mom and Dad rushed to them, their gaze fixed on Tommy, who was a few steps ahead. "What happened? Why's Tommy all wet?"

Tommy reached for his grandpa and recounted how Cass saved his hat. Jake filled them in on the rest.

Jen stopped Sam before they caught up to the others. "I think it would be better if Cass and I stop hanging out with you and your family for the rest of the cruise."

Warmth flooded his chest despite her words. He clasped her hand. "Not going to happen."

"But Jake's pretty mad. I don't want to be the cause of your family's special vacation being—"

Sam cut off her protest with a kiss. Her lips yielded to his, warm, sweet, inviting, shifting his world on its axis. Remembering where they were, he reluctantly pulled back and repeated firmly, "*Not* going to happen."

"But—"

Sam pressed a finger to her lips, enjoying how soft her eyes became. "Jake was just scared."

Tommy stared at them from his grandpa's shoulders, his eyes as round as beach balls. "You marrying Auntie Jen, Uncle Sam?"

Sam's heart backflipped into his throat. "*Auntie* Jen?" he managed to ask without stammering.

Mom let out a nervous laugh, her cheeks pink. At his raised eyebrow, she argued, "Two Miss Robbinses was too confusing for him."

"Well?" Tommy pressed, to which Jen giggled.

So much for the diversion tactic. Sam muffed Tommy's hair. "Kissing a girl doesn't always mean you'll marry her."

"But Gran said—"

Sam's dad slid his hand over Tommy's mouth. "How about a brownie, Champ?"

Sam turned back to his mother and the pink in her cheeks deepened to cherry red.

She fluttered her hand. "I might've said, 'Wouldn't it be nice…'"

"Uh-huh."

Suddenly, Jen's cheeks matched his mom's, and for a moment only the drone of a floatplane circling overhead and the distant hum of passengers broke the silence.

"Um." Cass burrowed deeper into the coat Jen had thrown over her shoulders. A puddle had formed on the walk at her feet. "Tommy and I really do need to get into dry clothes."

Jake picked at his own shirt, damp from holding Tommy. "Yeah, I think we all do."

Back at their cabin, Jake went straight to changing Tommy's clothes without uttering a word to Sam about the incident.

"I know you're angry, Jake, but—"

Jake silenced him with a glare then shuffled Tommy off to their parents' cabin with the mention of the brownie Grandpa had promised. The sugar-sweet voice disappeared the instant he returned. "This ends tonight."

"Ends? How? Tommy calls Cass *Auntie!* They have a room next door. You can't seriously think we're going to be able to avoid them for the rest of the cruise?"

Jake scrubbed a hand over his face, which was probably the closest he'd get to acknowledging Sam was right. "You put us in danger by hoodwinking us into this trip. You put *my son* in danger. How could you?"

"Jake, I'm sorry. If I'd had any idea someone was out to get Jennifer, I never would have involved the family. You must know that. It was supposed to be a simple fact-finding assignment."

Jake's gaze snapped to Sam's. "So you admit the tumble in the water *wasn't* an accident?"

"I doubt it." His boss would be livid if he knew how much Jake had already figured out, but after what happened to Tommy, Jake needed to know or they risked something worse happening. "When Jen and I got back to the cabin, there was a note waiting for them from their uncle, asking to meet on the pier."

"The 'uncle' that reporter said disappeared? He's here? And you think he pushed Cass in?"

"Mistakenly, I suspect. To be honest, I don't think Cass is entirely innocent."

"What?" Jake's eyes burned into him like laser beams. "You're telling me you let me and my son hang around with a suspect? A criminal?"

Sam sucked in a breath. Their father was supposed to be keeping an eye on her.

His brother's voice edged higher. "Suspected of doing what?"

"You know I can't tell you that. But Cass may have faked being pushed to avert suspicion from herself."

"With my son? No way! I don't believe it."

Sam pressed his lips into a grim line. Could he really see Cass putting Tommy in danger to clear her name?

His heart thumped. He suspected the woman of hiring someone to eliminate Jen. If she'd do that, she'd have few qualms about jumping in the water with Tommy. "She's a champion swimmer," he said evenly. "She could've reasoned he'd never be in real danger." And going in with Tommy made it look less likely it was deliberate. Scooping the boy into her arms in the first place had been completely out of character.

"You really think that—" Jake drilled a finger into Sam's shoulder "—and you didn't warn me! The woman is Tommy's new best friend."

"Jake, I'm sorry. She wasn't good with kids. I honestly didn't think the attraction would last."

"You didn't think is right." Jake withdrew his finger and paced the cabin, which seemed to be shrinking by the second. "What a mess. I warned you this would happen."

"You're right. The family is better off without me around." If he hadn't shown up at that family picnic all those years ago, Jimmy would still be alive.

"Don't even go there. This is about working a case on our family vacation. This is *not* about you being to blame for Jimmy's death. Don't you think it's time to get over yourself and accept the good that life has to offer and that's right in front of you?" Jake rubbed the bare place where his wedding band used to sit. "We all feel responsible for Jimmy, but checking out is just selfish."

The words twisted in Sam's chest like a knife. He stumbled backward. His legs hit the sofa and he sunk to the seat. Was that what the family thought of him?

"Cass isn't the only one Tommy's calling Auntie. Mom's probably mentally picking out wedding invitations for you and Jen as we speak."

"Right." Sam snorted. How much more could he let his family down? "Jen seemed cool with Tommy's question." And it didn't matter if his family thought he was selfish. They were safer without him around. Today proved it.

"What did you expect her to say after your lame answer?"

Sam cringed. He hadn't meant to hurt her feelings.

"Wait a second." Jake abruptly stopped. "You said you think Cass was trying to divert suspicion off herself by going in the water?"

"Yeah…"

"So why'd she say *the crowd* pushed her?"

"She probably thought I'd assume it was deliberate, so not saying so makes her look all the more innocent."

"Ever think that maybe she's looking so innocent because she is?"

Sam clutched a throw pillow and let his gaze drift to the glass door and the pier beyond. He blew out a breath. "Yeah, it's possible." But with Jen's life at stake, he wasn't taking any chances.

"I get it." The hard look in Jake's eyes slipped away. The tension in his voice dissolved. "You're falling for Jen. I mean really falling. Falling harder than you've ever fallen for anyone. You know, you're allowed to be happy."

Sam's mouth dried, even as his hands grew slick, but no way would he betray how close Jake had gotten to the truth. "I'm doing my job. Don't read more into this than there is."

"You're *not* doing your job. I know what you do. You win the trust of crooked art dealers, convince them to sell you something illegal, then arrest them for it."

Yeah, that about summed up his undercover gigs. *Befriend, then betray.* Not much of a way to live, when he thought about it. But in the process, the FBI art crime team had given America back millions of dollars in stolen national treasures—the battle flag of the Twelfth Regiment Infantry, Corps d'Afrique, a missing Rockwell painting. And not just American treasures. They'd returned a Rousseau taken from the home of a private collector in southern France, a Degas pastel stolen from an exhibit in Marseille, a Monet lifted from a Rotterdam museum.

As if Jake's throat had parched along with Sam's, Jake opened the fridge and took a swig from a water bottle. "But the brother I know—" Jake took his time twisting the lid back on the bottle and Sam's insides twisted right along with it "—wouldn't kiss a woman he planned to betray, let alone kiss her like you kissed Jen out there on the pier."

Sam ground his teeth to bite back words he knew he'd regret. Jake had no clue what it was like to work undercover. You did what had to be done. But even as he thought it, Sam had to concede that in Jen's case the rules didn't apply. Nothing he'd done had been because he was thinking of the case first. He'd been singularly focused on her welfare.

"Face it. You're too close." Jake jabbed the bottle toward Sam for added emphasis. "And it's skewing your perspective."

"Leave it alone."

Jake got into Sam's face. "I'm in the middle of this whether I like it or not, thanks to you. So don't tell me to leave it alone. You came aboard to do a job, but you're going to have to decide who you want to be— the *agent* that saves Jen's life and clears her name, or her shipboard romance."

He could be both, but Sam knew what Jake meant. If he didn't come clean, a fleeting shipboard romance was all there'd ever be between him and Jen. Trouble was, if he came clean, he could lose her anyway. "She'll be furious with me if I tell her the truth."

He shook his head. Was he actually contemplating the possibility? Their sting in Skagway hadn't worked, and their Jennifer-approved search of the Robbins gallery hadn't yielded a shred of evidence, either. He was running out of options if he wanted to nail Reggie and whoever else was involved. And there was no question he did. If he returned to Boston without finishing this, his gut told him Jen wouldn't see her twenty-sixth birthday.

"Oh, yeah, she'll be furious." Jake had the nerve to chuckle. "But if she loves you as much as I think she does, she'll get over it."

Sam's heart did a slow roll through his chest. *Now* Jake actually thought Jen loved him? Sam hugged the throw pillow he didn't remember burying his fingers into. Even if she loved him now, she wouldn't after he arrested her beloved guardian, and possibly her sister. What was he saying? There was no way he could trust her to keep his identity from Cass. Coming clean *wasn't* an option.

Jake tore the pillow from Sam's arms, an if-you-don't-I-will glint in his eyes. "Coming clean is your *only* option."

FIFTEEN

"Cass, wait!"

At the sound of Jen's cry, Sam jerked open his cabin door to find Cass hurrying down the hall and Jen, halfway out their door, yanking on her coat. "What's going on?"

"I told her about Reggie's note. She wants to find him before the ship leaves."

Sam glanced at his watch. "They'll be barring the exit in a few minutes."

"I know." Jen took off in the direction Cass had headed. "That's why I have to stop her."

"I've got to go," he called to his brother and then jogged after Jen. "Did she get another text from him?"

"Yes. It said, I'm sorry I missed you. That's what prompted me to tell her why we'd gone back out to the pier." Jen skidded to a stop as the elevator door shut her out. She slapped the down button. "After Tommy and Cass fell into the water, I hadn't exactly wanted to hang around out there, but Cass dashed out before I could tell her his note said he'd lost his phone so that wasn't Uncle Reggie texting."

The elevator doors swept open and Jen plunged inside with Sam on her heels. He'd had the local PD scouring the pier and surrounding area for their elusive uncle for more than an hour after his nephew's near drowning, but they hadn't spotted him. He doubted the man had ever intended to show himself. Sam should've given the police the number Cass had been calling and seen if they could triangulate the signal.

The elevator ground to a stop at every deck, gaining an extra couple passengers at each. When they finally reached the disembarkation level, Jen was more antsy to get out than a cat in a dog pen.

"There she is!" Jen pointed to the exit where Cass was arguing with a petite female crew member as her brawny male counterpart blocked the exit.

"The door is only still open, ma'am, because one of the tour excursion buses is late returning." The crew member pointed to the printed schedule that each passenger received every morning. "Passengers are no longer permitted to leave. The time is clearly stated. If I let you leave, I'd have to let anyone else who asked. I'm sorry."

"But you don't understand," Cass pleaded as he and Jen reached her side. "My uncle came all this way to see us."

Jen seemed relieved that the crew member wasn't giving in, and Sam continued to wonder if Cass had more sinister motives for not wanting to miss seeing her uncle.

"If you hurry to the open deck," the crew member suggested, "you might be able to wave to him."

With scarcely a glance in their direction, Cass raced for the spiral staircase. "I can't believe you didn't tell me about the note sooner," Cass griped as he and Jen caught up to her.

"Cass, something weird is going on. Reg's note said he lost his phone."

"What? Then who's been texting me?" She reached in her jacket pocket, but her hand came out empty. "Great, I must've left my phone in the cabin. Reg probably found his again after he left the note is all."

Jen met Sam's gaze, and he shrugged. It was a reasonable explanation. Except… "Don't you think he would've mentioned the note in his texts then?" Sam asked, not sure whose side he hoped to help by the question. If Reggie had wanted it to look like the text messages came from someone else, he wouldn't have mentioned the note, any more than someone else would have. Considering how soon she'd contacted him by phone after their tour bus pulled away, he'd have had to lose his phone between texting her and walking to the ship, then found it again before they arrived for their rendezvous at Creek Street. Not so believable.

From the anxiousness on Jen's face, he suspected she was thinking along the same lines. He could use that uncertainty to his advantage if he admitted to her he was with the FBI and stressed how important it was to not say anything to Cass since her loyalties clearly lay with their uncle.

Cass pushed past a group blocking the door to the open deck and burst outside. She ran along the railing and scanned the near-empty pier. "Do you see him? I don't see him."

"He probably gave up waiting for us a long time ago," Jen said tiredly. "Certainly after the ship shut its doors."

Cass visibly deflated. "Yeah, I guess you're right. I feel so bad that he came all this way to surprise us and we missed him."

"If seeing us had been his priority, he would've cut short his meeting this afternoon, don't you think?" Jen edged a sheepish look Sam's way as if seeking moral support.

Oh, man, she was clearly struggling to know what to believe. Would there ever be a more perfect opportunity to come clean? If he could convince her to cooperate in a sting, he could get her the answers she craved once and for all.

"I think you're being too hard on him." Cass shivered. "I'm going to take a hot shower. I'm still chilled from that dunk in the water. You coming back to the cabin?"

"I—"

Sam caught Jen's hand before she could finish answering. "How about taking a walk around the deck with me?"

Cass waved. "I'll see you two later."

Sam led Jen to a secluded section of the deck.

"I can't believe how paranoid you've made me.

Now you've got me questioning who sent those text messages."

Sam stroked his thumb over the back of her fingers, struggling with how to begin. "Paranoia is good. It'll keep you alive."

She shuddered. "I tried to remember if maybe that redhead, Bellamy's roommate, was in the crowd when Cass and Tommy went off the dock. Did you notice?"

Sam tried to recall the crowd. He'd been so intent on getting to Tommy that he hadn't paid enough attention. "No, I didn't. I'm sorry."

She swallowed so loudly he heard the gulp. "What am I going to do when I'm back in Seattle? How can I protect myself when I don't even know who's really after me? Was Bellamy acting alone? Or is there still someone else out there who wants to get rid of me?"

Sam stepped to the rail and drew her close. "I think I have a plan that would compel your uncle to confess, but you'd have to promise not to say anything to Cass."

"I can't believe she's involved in anything illegal."

"But we don't know for sure," Sam reminded her. "So we can't risk it."

"But wouldn't we be risking her safety?"

"If you both died—" Jen paled and Sam curled his arm around her shoulder "—your uncle would lose control of the gallery. If he wants to keep doing what he's doing, he needs one of you alive. You don't want the gallery, but Cass does. And he can control her, keep doing what he's been doing, maybe without her suspecting a thing or maybe with her full knowledge."

"But this plan of yours, does it involve the police?"

"The FBI."

Her widening eyes rivaled Tommy's earlier gawk. "Why? You plan to let Reg kidnap me?"

"No, because of the art crime connection."

She met his gaze and the trust mingled with trepidation in her eyes heaped burning coals on his chest. "I guess you've worked with them before if you've handled security for art galleries."

"Yeah." Sam waited as a couple passed by, then lowered his voice. "Jen, I haven't been completely honest with you about my job because I didn't know if you were party to your uncle's alleged deals." His guts churned.

She stiffened, her forehead furrowing. "You thought I'd sell stolen paintings?"

The hurt in her voice cut to the core. The wind whipped strands of hair across her face and he tucked them behind her ear, letting his fingers linger on her cheek. "Not once I got to know you."

"But I didn't tell you about the paintings until—" She let out a strangled sound. "What are you saying?"

He drew a deep breath. "I'm an FBI agent. We had reason to believe that Michaels sent you and your sister on this cruise to collect a stolen painting and bring it back to Seattle."

What little color she'd had left drained from her face. "From the gallery in Skagway..." She backed out of his reach. "That's why you wanted to come with us. The whole way there, I felt like people were watching us. And they were, weren't they?"

"Yes."

"So none of this was real?" Her voice broke. "You were just playing me."

"No, I mean, yes." He shook his head and clasped her upper arms. "Yes, I was supposed to win your trust, but my feelings for you are real, Jen. You have to believe me. If they weren't, I wouldn't be telling you any of this. I would have walked away at the end of this cruise and you would have been none the wiser."

She cupped her hand over her mouth, looking so much like she wanted to believe him. "Does your family know?"

"No, I never told them."

"But Jake knows. That's what he meant, isn't it? When he said this has gone too far?"

Sam exhaled. "Yes. He figured it out."

"I can't believe I sided with you over Cass. She warned me. She said it was weird how the police would feed you all this information and how you seemed to know everything." Jen's voice grew fainter with each word and, backing away from him, she had this panicked deer-caught-in-the-headlights look. "How could you? I thought you were different! Sharing this cruise with your family has been—" She gulped. "I thought you actually cared about me."

He reached out to her but let his hands drop back to his sides when she cringed at his touch. "I do care, Jen."

"You don't. You just care about what you could get from me—like every other guy I ever dated."

The comparison stung.

"I don't want to be like them, Jen. You have to be-lieve me." He was slimier than fish bait for romanc-ing her the way he had, but he needed to turn this around and fast. "That's why I had to tell you, be-cause I don't want to walk away from you at the end of this cruise. I want to help you."

"Help me? You've ruined everything. All I ever wanted was to have a quiet family life." Her voice edged higher. "But no one will ever buy the gallery after you drag it through the mud. I'll never escape."

He clasped her arm and maneuvered them farther away from the others on deck. "You can't escape by running." The sudden memory of his aunt and uncle's grief-stricken faces at Jimmy's grave caught him in the gut. *Who was he to lecture anyone about not running from troubles?* Not that he'd been run-ning so much as staying away for his family's sake. He'd let them down enough for one lifetime.

Jen folded her arms and glared. "You have no idea what it's like to have your life dissected in print. If you'd had to endure the malicious speculations the newspapers entertained after my parents died, you'd understand why I couldn't go to the police."

"I'm sorry." His heart ached at how much that ex-perience had clearly cost her. But he still needed to convince her to work with him.

"It was never about the money." Her hand inched up to her throat and captured the cross pendant dan-gling there. "I was going to drown if I didn't get out."

A warning horn sounded from the ship's bridge

and Sam motioned to the windows overlooking the deck, where the captain stood. "Do you know what sailors do when a storm threatens to tear their ship apart?"

She stared at him mutely.

"They throw their excess cargo overboard—everything—and cling to what matters...the ship." He stroked his thumb over her hand that still clutched the cross at her throat. "God is our ship, Jen. Don't you think maybe it's time for you to cling to *Him?* And consider that he might have sent me here to protect you?"

Sitting on the lounge chair on her cabin's balcony, Jen unfolded the picture Tommy had given her their first day at sea. Her heart clenched at the sight of the little stick family standing alongside her on the ship's bow. To be part of a family like Sam's again had been all she'd ever wanted. She traced the faces, and when she reached her own, a tear dribbled from her chin, smearing the wide smile Tommy had given her.

She swiped at her damp cheek. She should've listened when Sam told Tommy that kissing a girl didn't always mean you'd marry her. Except that his kiss had seemed to make promises beyond words. And then when Tommy called her "Auntie," Sam's eyes had gone soft, as if the name appealed to him.

The balcony door slid open and Jen hurriedly stuffed the picture back into her Bible as Cass stepped out.

"I don't get you. You obviously really like Sam.

His family is great. He's even a believer, which is so important to you. So what's the problem?"

"Just let it go. Okay, Cass?"

"Not this time."

"What's that supposed to mean?"

Cass winced.

Jen's heart took a nervous dip. "Cass?"

"Ian's been asking me if there's any chance you'd take him back."

"What?" *The emails.*

"He says he misses you. That he was more offended that you let Reggie do the dirty work than ask him yourself. He says he'll sign a prenup."

"And you believed him?"

"Yeah, but I didn't tell you because I think you were more in love with the idea of the family you'd make with him than with Ian himself. You never glowed around him like you do around Sam."

Tears clogged Jen's throat. She covered her mouth, shook her head. It was true because deep down she'd never really trusted that Ian loved her for herself.

"Look, Sam practically accused me of dealing stolen art. He shouldn't be on my most-want-to-hangout-with-my-sister list. But he makes you happy. At least he did up until twenty-four hours ago. Why can't you forgive him for whatever stupid thing he said or did?"

"It's not that simple."

"Uh, yeah, it is." She leaned back against the railing and crossed her arms. "Isn't forgiving people one of the Ten Commandments or something?"

"No." Jen clutched her Bible to her chest and stared at the rippling water. If Cass knew Sam was asking her to help get evidence against Uncle Reggie and maybe her, too, she'd be singing a different tune. Sam might have said he didn't want to be like the other men who'd betrayed her, but he was. If he hadn't wanted to get inside information on her uncle, would he have given her a second look?

"I don't know why you cling so tightly to that Bible." Cass jerked her nose toward it. "It doesn't seem to make you any happier."

Jen gasped, disbelief razoring her throat.

"I mean, those hymns we used to sing, when Mom and Dad dragged us to church, said living in the spirit gives you peace, right?"

Jen gaped. That's what the scripture said, too. So why didn't she feel it?

She'd always hoped escaping the gallery, making a home, a family, away from the limelight would give her peace...one day.

My peace I give you.

Her heart quickened at the scripture that flitted through her mind. Was Sam right about her? That she wasn't clinging to God?

Her fingers tightened around the Bible. She'd been praying He'd help her sell the gallery and realize her dreams, never once considering that *her* dreams might not be what *He* wanted for her.

A knock sounded at the cabin door.

Cass pushed herself off the rail. "I'll get it." After stepping inside, she poked her head back out to the balcony. "Remember what Mom used to say—there isn't a man alive who can bring you happiness if you don't know how to be happy on your own."

The words hit Jen like a punch to the gut. "Oh, Lord, is that my problem? Have I been looking to others to make me happy?"

Cass reappeared too soon. "There's someone here who wants to talk to you."

Jen sprang to her feet and backed toward the rail. "Oh, Cass, no." How could she do this to her? "I don't want to talk to him."

Jake poked his head out the door. "I don't blame you."

"Jake? I thought—" She pressed a hand to her hammering heart. "Never mind."

Anguish creased Jake's face. "Jen, I want to apologize."

"You?" Jen lowered her hand. "For what?"

"For what I said on the pier yesterday. Clearly, I made you feel like you needed to stay away from us because of the danger you've been in."

"Oh, no, I—" Remembering her promise not to repeat Sam's secret, she clamped her mouth shut. She'd lost count of how many times she'd bit back the words that would've at least made Cass understand why she was avoiding Sam. Did Jake really think his outburst was the reason?

"I didn't mean to make you feel like you were in any way to blame," Jake went on. "I don't want you to feel self-conscious around the family. We all care about you and miss you."

"See-ee-ee," Cass said.

Jen pressed her lips harder to keep from letting her emotions escape.

"Sam misses you most of all," Jake added.

A bubble of hurt burbled up her chest and came out in a moan.

"C'mon, Jen," Cass scolded. "I am not going to let you spend another day moping around the cabin. It's our last day aboard. It's our birthday!"

"Yes." Jake caught Jen's hand and tugged. "And we want to help you and Cass celebrate."

Jen managed a small smile. Funny how she'd spent the past few years dreamily looking forward to this day, when her future would finally be hers to choose.

Nothing had worked out as she'd hoped. She traced the decorative swirls in the cross at her neck—surface decorations. It was time she truly lived in the faith she professed and embraced God's plans for her. No one could ever love her more.

After an afternoon of Ping-Pong matches and board games with the Steele family, a delicious dinner together and an evening of entertainment in the ship's theatre, Jen closed her eyes against the brightly lit stage and the closing night's high-octane musical. For the first time in longer than she could remember, maybe ever, she'd enjoyed just being with people without expectations or wishful thinking or being suspicious of ulterior motives.

For the first time, she'd known to the depths of her being that Christ's love was the love she'd been yearning for all these years. And that no romantic love or family love or any other kind could satisfy her more completely, or more unfailingly.

She leaned over to her sister in the darkened theater. "Thanks for talking me into joining the fun."

Cass winked. "You're welcome." She tilted her head toward Sam in the row ahead of them and mouthed "talk to him."

He was cuddling Tommy on his lap—he was the picture of everything she'd ever hoped for in a man. Well, except for his wanting to arrest her sister and uncle and lying to her.

They hadn't revisited yesterday's revelation or his request for her help. There hadn't been any opportunity. Thank goodness, because although he'd convinced her that she needed to cling to God, she didn't think she could do what Sam wanted. He'd have to get his evidence some other way.

The instant Jake lifted Tommy from Sam's arms, Sam reached over his seat back and caught her hand. "We need to talk."

Her pulse quickened.

Cass gave her an I'm-behind-you hug. "I'll see you later."

He waited for his family and the other theatergoers to file out, giving her too much time to remember how much she enjoyed holding his hand.

"I know you just came out today for your sister and my family. You have every right to hate me. But I can't walk away until I'm sure you'll be safe."

Her heart stuttered. *He was walking away.* She

swallowed her disappointment. "I don't see what more you can do. Now that my suspicions are out of the bag, I'm sure that if Reggie had anything to do with the attacks, he'll back off and be more than happy to buy me out."

Sam glanced around the now empty theatre. "I'm not so sure."

She shivered at the ominous undertone to his words.

"What you said yesterday, about the newspaper stories after your parents' deaths, got me thinking that all this might go back a lot further than we thought."

Her breath caught in her throat. Was this another ploy to get her to cooperate in whatever scheme he'd dreamed up now to trap her uncle?

"While you were holed up in your cabin yesterday, I dug into those stories."

The corners of Jen's cross pendant dug into her palm. The papers had published rumors that her parents had been involved in unscrupulous deals and that maybe some underworld figure had bumped them off because they didn't deliver. She strained to breathe. It wasn't true. How could Sam dredge up those horrible lies?

"I think Reginald Michaels had already been using your parents' gallery as a cover for fraudulent deals before their deaths," Sam whispered. "Only, they figured it out, told him 'we can't go on like this.'"

We can't go on like this. Jen's pent-up breath escaped in a rush. *It was* Reggie, of course. She'd buried memories of those horrible accusations so deep, she hadn't made the connection. "That's what Mom meant!"

"What are you talking about?"

"Mom kept a journal. The day she died she wrote, *We plan to confront him tonight, and hope that will be the end of it. We can't go on like this.*"

"I didn't find any mention of a journal in the police file."

Jen covered her mouth and shook her head. "With the speculation of a mob connection in the news, I was afraid the journal entry would make my parents look guilty, when I knew they weren't." Only deep down she'd worried they were.

"So your parents must have confronted Reginald after the gala, and maybe his fear of arrest drove him to kill them before that could happen. The medical examiner's report said they both suffered multiple blows to the head." Sam clasped her hand. "They were attributed to the airbag deflating after initial impact, allowing their heads to hit the dash as the car careened down the ridge. But someone could have followed the car down—" he hesitated, compassion glistening in his eyes "—and finished the job."

The image of Uncle Reggie slamming Mom's head into the dash crushed Jen's chest. "You think Reggie killed my parents?"

SIXTEEN

Sitting in the Bordeaux dining room, waiting for his family's turn to disembark, Sam glanced at his watch for the tenth time. Monticello had been scheduled to leave the ship thirty minutes ago. Sam should've received an update by now on the search.

As if on cue, his phone rang.

He punched Talk. "Well?"

"He's clean," the FBI agent on the other end reported. "Seemed smug about the search, though, as if he'd known we'd be there."

"Okay, you know what to do."

"Yeah, Agent Moore just boarded. The Captain's summoned the art gallery staff."

Sam wished he could interrogate them, but he couldn't afford to blow his cover around anyone in the art world—Jen being his one exception.

"Anything?" she asked, her expression tight.

He shook his head.

Cass and Jake, even his parents, seemed to watch them with eagle eyes. Jen was doing her best to look like they'd made up, but this whole ruse obviously had her too on edge.

Sam leaned close and whispered in her ear. "It'll be over soon. I promise. But if you want Cass to buy my spending a few extra days in town, you need to look happier about it."

Jen smiled and slanted a shy glance Cass's direction that even Sam almost believed.

"You may now proceed to the exit," the crew member in charge of their waiting area announced.

Jen clasped Sam's hand. "This is it."

Except as they made their way through customs, there was no sign of Reggie waiting to meet them as expected.

"There's Blake!" Cass pointed to a tall, dark-haired man Sam recognized from his file.

Blake swept Cass into his arms. "Welcome home!"

Sam caught Jake's gaze, wondering how he felt about the more-than-friendly greeting.

Jake shrugged as if he hadn't expected anything different.

That was one plus, anyway.

"Where's Uncle Reggie?" Jen asked after Cass made the introductions. "I thought he was meeting us."

"Yeah, I don't know what's wrong with him. Well, I guess you know that he flew to Alaska to surprise you girls. But then he got sick before he found you."

"Sick?" Cass shot Jen a worried look. "Is he going to be okay?"

"Sure, nothing keeps Dad down for long. He says

he'll see you—" Blake snaked his arm around Cass's waist and nuzzled her neck "—at the gallery first thing tomorrow morning, and both of you tomorrow night for a belated birthday dinner."

Collecting his and Jen's luggage, Sam studied the interplay between Cass and Blake, still not certain he could trust either of them.

The air was unusually sticky for early July in Seattle, much like the air between him and Jen ever since she'd agreed to his plan to ferret out whoever was behind the smuggling and attacks. Parked a block from the gallery, Sam checked the wire he'd fitted on her, then double-checked that his men were in position.

"The courier is heading up the street now," a fellow agent's voice came over the mic fitted in Sam's ear.

"Okay, you ready?" Sam asked Jen. At her breathless nod, he opened her door. "You remember the signal?"

"I twist my nose." She demonstrated then scrunched her nose. "It's kind of obvious, don't you think?"

"Better than using something you might do unintentionally, like fiddling with your necklace." He nodded toward her hand doing just that.

"Oh." She dropped her hand. "I see what you mean."

His pulse raced more than usual when moving in on a sting. He'd never put anyone other than criminals or law enforcement officers on the front line. If his boss knew what she meant to him, he'd never have agreed to the setup, but he couldn't think of any other way to expediently protect Jen from Michaels.

He caught her hand as they approached the gallery's front door. "Think you can manage to convince him you're head over heels in love with me?"

For the first time in two days she treated him to a smile that actually reached her eyes. "Yeah, I think I can handle that." The faint blush that bloomed in her cheeks renewed his hope that feelings for him still lingered in her heart. He couldn't resist leaning close and brushing a kiss across her sweet dimple as they stopped at the glass door. He was, after all, supposed to be madly in love with her. Not that he had to pretend.

They intercepted the courier at the door. Jen signed for the package—the unsold auction item returned from the ship.

The bell above the door jingled as they stepped inside. Sam scanned the showroom for customers and cataloged the entry points. "Clear," he murmured for the benefit of those listening in, as Jen set the package on the counter.

Reginald Michaels emerged from the back room. "Jen! Good to see you. Cass told me you might drop by. So…" He pulled Jen into a hug then looked Sam over. "Is this the young man your sister has been gushing about?"

Jen clutched Sam's arm and leaned close, gifting him with a whiff of her floral fragrance. "This is my Sam."

His heart shifted at the description, and he was

so caught up in watching her expression that it took him a second to meet Reggie's offered hand. "Good to meet you, sir."

"Sam's interested in buying a painting I told him about. He thinks it would suit one of his clients' décor."

"Oh?" Reggie returned his attention to Sam. "What do you do for a living?"

"I'm in security."

"How interesting." Reggie's gaze strayed briefly to the unopened package. "So what painting were you considering?"

"Jen described it as a duel between two men in masquerade."

Reggie's brow creased, but Sam didn't miss the panic that flickered in his gaze as his attention returned to Jen. "I'm not sure what piece you mean. I don't think we have anything like that."

"Sure we do. I saw it in the storage room."

"I'm afraid you're mistaken." He turned to Sam. "Is there something else that might interest you?"

"No, Uncle Reggie, you must remember it. A dueler in a white jester's costume, blood staining his shirt, fallen into the arms of his double."

The image sent a chill straight to Sam's bones, and suddenly the idea of leaving Jen alone to continue the duel with her uncle didn't sound like a good one at all.

But he stuck to the plan and gave her a sideways hug and peck on the cheek. "That's okay. It would've looked great in the theatre's lobby, but if you don't have it, you don't have it. I need to run those errands. I'll pick you up in an hour?"

Jen let out an authentic-sounding humph. "I'll be here."

Sam hurried to the command post—a painter's truck positioned two stores down—and climbed in on the side not visible from the gallery. "She on camera?" With Jen's permission, they'd secretly tapped into the gallery's surveillance feed.

"Shh," the agent monitoring audio hissed.

"Jen, what are you doing, telling your boyfriend about paintings you found in a back room?" Reginald barked.

Jen gave him a strange look. "Because we're in the business of selling paintings."

"You don't even work here."

"But as you so often remind me, a co-owner needs to put in an appearance now and then."

Another member of Sam's team poked his head into the van. "I cross-referenced the son's phone records like you asked. You were right. Blake has a few suspicious contacts."

"Good work. Find out everything you can on them. I want every angle on this case followed up on." Sam returned his attention to Reggie's voice on the audio feed.

"Stick to selling the art that's hanging on the wall."

"Why? He was willing to pay a good price for that piece." Jen moved out of camera view for a moment then appeared on the next screen, tapping on the store's computer. "Maybe the guy who bought it from you would be interested in selling." She scanned the computer screen, tapping keys every few seconds. Her shoulders sagged. "There's no record of the sale."

Reggie folded his arm over his chest. "Because I never owned it."

"I know what I saw."

"Why don't you stick to assessing grant applications and let me worry about the gallery?"

"You'd like that, wouldn't you?" Jen sounded on the verge of tears. "Because Cass is easier to dupe."

"What?"

"I saw that painting in the storage room two weeks ago. If it's not here now, and there's no record of its sale, then you must have sold it and pocketed the money for yourself."

"You're talking crazy."

"Am I? Then where's the sales receipt? And how do you explain this?" Jen tore the brown paper off the unsold painting returned from the ship—the painting that an employee of the ship's gallery had used to conceal the stolen one in return for a quick two hundred bucks from a man fitting the description of Sal Monticello.

Sam smiled at Reggie's increasing edginess.

"How'd she get in there?" The agent monitoring the panel pointed to camera three.

Sam bit back an expletive at the sight of Cass emerging from the back room. "I thought you said she left."

"She did."

"Did Mom and Dad figure out you were fencing

stolen art?" Cass pulled a gun from her pocket and pointed it at Reggie's chest. "Their accident was no *accident,* was it?"

At Jen's gasp, Sam's heart rammed into his rib cage.

Cass glanced toward the front window then with a wave of the weapon forced Reggie and Jen to move to the office.

Sam ran toward the front door as voices over his earpiece tallied the new positions taken by his team members.

"Shut up and let me listen," he growled into his mic, watching on his cell phone the view from the button cam he'd fitted to Jen's shirt as he slipped inside the gallery, careful not to sound the door's overhead bell.

Reggie's hands had shot into the air. "Of course it was an accident. Your father was like a brother to me. I never would have hurt him."

"But you'd hire Bellamy to hurt Jen?" Cass pulled back the gun's hammer.

"Cass, what are you doing?" Jen stepped in front of the gun.

Sam's heart climbed to his throat.

"Don't do this," she pleaded.

"I swear it wasn't me." Reggie's voice tickled soprano. "I'd never let anyone hurt Jen or you. You are like daughters to me."

Shaking her head, Cass sidestepped, reclaiming her bead on Reggie. "I should've believed you, Jen."

Reggie edged toward the door.

Cass tracked his movement with her gun. "You're not going anywhere until you tell us the truth."

Sam didn't like the way her finger stroked the trigger.

"You've got it all wrong," Reginald said.

"Then, by all means, enlighten us."

Sam stood mesmerized outside the office door and motioned his partner to stay back. Cass's crazy plan might just work.

"Sniper in position."

Sam's blood ran cold at the announcement that blasted through his earpiece. "Stand down," he hissed. "She's on our side." He hoped.

"Threatening to kill the suspect was not in the plan," his cohort shot back.

Lord, Jen will never forgive me if anything happens to her sister. Sam holstered his weapon and rushed into the room. He didn't care what it cost him. Jen and Cass weren't going to pay for his stupid theory. Sighting the sniper's line of fire through the window, he stepped into it, his gaze fixed on Cass. "You don't want to do this."

"Yes, I do."

"You?" Reggie croaked. "Who are you? A cop?"

"What are you doing?" blared over Sam's earpiece. "Move."

Sam yanked the piece from his ear and held his hands up, palms out, standing his ground between Cass and their sniper. "Cass, please don't do this. We don't know that Reggie killed your parents."

"I didn't," Reggie repeated.

"Cass, listen to him," Jen urged.

"I told Jen that to convince her to help me," Sam added.

Tears streamed down Cass's cheeks, but her sights never left the end of her barrel. "Why should I believe you now?"

"Because I just kissed my job goodbye by walking into my sniper's line of fire."

She snorted. "You should've let him shoot."

"I couldn't." Sam signaled his partner to pull Jen out of harm's way, then took a step closer to Cass. "He's aiming at you."

Jen gasped at the sniper's red dot picking off Cass's shoulder and fought against the agent's grip.

Sam held out his hand palm up. "Please, hand me the gun."

"Cass, give Sam the gun!"

Sam inched closer, his palm still up, and the red dot jumped to his back.

"Cass, give him the gun!" The empathetic look Sam shot Jen tore at her heart.

The air grew thicker with every tick of the clock— the clock that she and Cass had given Mom and Dad for their twentieth anniversary…two weeks before their deaths.

Cass stiffened her stance. "Not until he confesses."

"A confession at gunpoint?" Sam chided. "You think a judge will accept it?"

"I don't care. I want to hear him say it."

"Cass, please," Jen begged. "I can't lose you, too."

Sweat slicked Uncle Reggie's brow, utter defeat twisting his face.

"I just want to know the truth."

"He killed your parents," said a familiar female voice.

Jen's gaze shot to the door. "Aunt Martha?"

Sam's attention jerked to the officer holding her arm. "What are you bringing her in here for?"

"If you'd kept your earpiece in, we could've told you."

Aunt Martha tossed Reggie a disgusted look. "He's a crook and a killer."

"No, Martha, you're wrong," Reggie pleaded. "I was trying to protect you."

"Sure." Aunt Martha turned her attention to Cass. "A month after you came to live with us, the guy he paid to run your parents off the road phoned to blackmail him for more money. I overheard the conversation on the extension. Reg threatened to kill him, too, if he ever went to the police or called again."

"Martha, no," Uncle Reggie protested. "I didn't hire him. I would never have done that to Ed and Katherine."

Aunt Martha clasped Jen's hand. "I was too afraid to confront him or go to the police. He'd fooled everyone, and if he went to jail, it would've only made your lives more difficult. So I did my best to take care of you girls."

Tears stung Jen's eyes. "That's why you divorced him as soon as we moved out?"

"Yes. I never told him what I knew. We'd drifted apart, and he never questioned my request. I'm sorry."

Reggie backed up a step and let his hands drop a few inches.

Cass locked her elbows, refocused on him. "Keep your hands in the air."

Jen ripped free of the agent's hold. "Cass, don't. We know what happened now. That's enough. Let the law deal with him."

"You're wrong," Uncle Reggie moaned.

Aunt Martha shook her head.

"I should have known you'd try something underhanded when Blake told me how antsy you were getting that Jen might try to sell the gallery." Aunt Martha swallowed and turned to her. "I didn't think he'd hurt you. If you both died, he'd lose everything. I never imagined he'd try to kill just you until Cass called this morning to ask what I knew about his business ethics."

Jen smiled at her sister. "You did that?"

Cass shrugged.

The officer who'd brought in Aunt Martha pulled handcuffs from his belt. "She also confirmed Bellamy was the name of his hired gun."

Cass glared down the barrel at Reggie. "How could you?"

The sniper's red dot appeared on her chest.

"No!" Sam lunged, shoving her arms skyward.

Jen dove to cover his back.

A loud click reverberated in her ears as they tumbled to the floor. Somehow Sam twisted midfall so that he landed on his back with Jen on top of him. The gun dropped to the tile with a thud and Sam swatted it toward an officer. "What did you think you were doing?"

"Stopping you from getting shot!"

Officers swarmed the room.

Still lying on the floor beneath Jen, Sam cradled her face between his palms, pressed a kiss to her lips, then clutched her to his chest. "You almost gave me a heart attack."

Beneath her ear, his heart thundered as strong as ever, and she gloried in the sound.

An officer pried her from his arms. Another held Cass and reached for the handcuffs at his hip.

Another officer tapped the opened barrel of Cass's gun to his palm. "It's empty."

Jen gaped at Cass. "Did you know?"

She grinned. "Of course."

Sam scrambled to his feet and stayed the officer's hand that was about to slap a cuff on Cass. "You don't need those. Take them to command post."

As the officer escorted them out, a man in a suit stormed toward Sam.

They stepped outside just as Blake pulled up in his car. He bolted out of his seat and raced to them. "Mom, Cass, what happened?"

Aunt Martha rushed into his arms. "It's your father."

Several news vans careened onto the street.

"Oh, no," Jen groaned.

"Just give me a minute." The officer escorting them stopped to cordon off the door with police tape.

Blake eyeballed the cameramen pouring out of the vans. "A minute will be too late. Get in my car."

"Good idea," Cass seconded, and they all scrambled into the black SUV with its tinted windows before a single reporter spotted them.

Instead the reporters pounced on the officer taping off the perimeter.

Blake started his car. "We'd better pull out of the way before those vultures clue in to us sitting here." He nosed the car past the news vans.

"Pull over here." From the backseat, Jen pointed to the command post, disguised as a painter's van.

Blake hung a left instead.

Twisting in her seat, Jen scrambled to see what prompted the change of course. "Blake, what are you doing?"

SEVENTEEN

Sam guided a handcuffed and subdued Reginald Michaels to the gallery's front door and groaned at the sight of news reporters—exactly what Jen had hoped to avoid.

The officer who'd escorted the women stepped inside. "You may want to slip out the back way."

Sam steered Michaels toward the rear of the store. "Where's Jennifer Robbins?"

"They jumped into their aunt's son's SUV to get away from the media. He drove—"

"What?" Panic streaked across Reggie's face. "You have to stop him. He's the killer, the thief. He hired Bellamy." The man started to sob. "Oh, what have I done?"

"Take him." Sam shoved Reggie to the officer and raced outside. News vans lined the street, not an SUV in sight. Heart hammering, he raced to the command post van and flung open the door. "Have you seen the women?"

"Not yet."

"Put out a BOLO on Blake Michaels's SUV." Sam

choked down the bile rising to his throat. If anything happened to— He cut off the thought and charged to the back of the gallery. Nothing was going to happen to her. He wouldn't let her down the way he'd let his family down. As Reggie stepped out the back door, Sam clutched his shoulders and shook him—hard. "Where did Blake take them?"

"He had a drug problem when he was young, owed bad guys a lot of money. He fenced a couple paintings to pay them. I didn't know! I swear, I didn't know." Michaels broke down again.

Sam tightened his grip. "Where did he take them?"

"Jen's parents figured it out and confronted him," Michaels rambled. "Told him to turn himself in or they would. But I didn't know any of that until Bellamy called, trying to blackmail *me*. That's what Martha overheard." Anguish squeezed his voice. "He's our son. Turning him in wouldn't have brought back their parents. It would only have broken his mother's heart."

"I don't care about that now. We have to find them."

"I took the girls in and gave them the best home I could," Michaels blubbered.

An agent burst out the gallery's back door, holding the earpiece Sam had torn out earlier. "I think you're going to want to hear this."

Sam snatched it up and pressed it to his ear. "I hear her. She can't be too far." He pulled his cell phone to view her button cam feed. "It's fuzz." He tapped the earpiece. Fuzz, too.

Out of range? His pulse escalated. Or did Blake

find the wire? "Play back the last audio you have and get a locate on her cell phone."

"On it."

Sam caught Reggie by the collar before the other officer could shove him into the waiting car. "Where would Blake take her?"

Agony creased the man's face. "I don't know."

Sam shoved him against the car. "Think!"

"He's got a plane."

"Where?"

"Stalwart."

Sam's heart ricocheted at the mention of his hometown. "There's no airport there."

"No, that's how he flew us to Alaska to meet the girls. I should've known he was up to his old tricks after I got sick. Didn't remember a thing between leaving a note with the ship's crew and getting home to my bed."

Sam gave Reg another hard shake. "Where's his plane?"

"A farmer lets him use his field."

The Johnsons. Next to his uncle's farm. Twenty minutes away, maybe longer, depending on traffic. He left Michaels to the officer and raced to command post. "I need to see that feed. How much of a head start are we talking?"

"Seven minutes." The tech guy hit Play on the feed and glanced at his watch. "Eight minutes."

"Get me a copter!" Sam strained to hear what Jen had said before they lost contact. *Why are you driving west on Nickerson?* "She was feeding us locations!"

"Helicopter is three minutes out. You need to meet them at the helipad," the agent reported.

"Get me the last location she mentions before the audio cuts out." Sam motioned two agents to follow him. "And get me that locate on her cell phone."

"Want roadblocks set up?"

"Not yet. Let him get onto Fifteenth first. Once he's on the bridge, there are no escape routes." Sam tossed his keys to his partner. "You drive. I've got a call to make."

As they sped toward the makeshift helipad, Sam got his dad on the line.

"Son, I saw the news. What can we do?"

Sam's heart crunched into his ribs. *We.* Not just Dad, the whole Steele clan. They'd always been there for him no matter what—just like Jake said—accepting his decision to move away, forgiving him for missing the reunions. *Lord, I should've been here for them, too. I've missed too many years by running. Please, don't let it be too late.*

"I knew the second you spotted the duelers' painting in the back room that you'd ruin everything," Blake growled, shooting a blistering glare at the rearview mirror.

Jen gripped the back of the seat as he squealed around the corner. "You were there?"

"Yeah, to pick it up. If you'd been ten minutes later..." He smacked the steering wheel. "I'd just pried it out of the piece disguising it when I heard you come in."

"So *you* speared that note to my car? To scare me out of reporting it? Or to scare me out of selling the gallery and destroying your little sideline?"

"No," Blake spat. "To scare you into taking the cruise. I figured your *accidental* death wouldn't be scrutinized as closely by the Alaskan authorities," he explained cooly, as if he didn't expect her to live to repeat it.

In the front seat beside him, Aunt Martha gasped. "It was you?"

Beside Jen on the backseat, Cass let out a choked sound. "You hired Bellamy?"

"Yeah." Blake tossed a smirk over his shoulder, ignoring his mother's horrified expression. "And when he got himself arrested, and you told me that the press was out for blood, I flew Dad to Juneau and Ketchikan to fix it myself. Dad had no idea what I was doing, of course." Blake snorted. "Thought I was reformed."

Jen caught Cassie's gaze and telegraphed an escape plan.

The instant Blake slowed his car for the stop sign, Jen silently unlatched her seat belt, and mouthed to Cass "Now!" Simultaneously, they grabbed the door handles. The doors wouldn't open.

Jen rammed her shoulder against hers, slapped the window with her hand. "Let us out." Jen knew that this was what Sam had feared. He'd never forgive himself if they didn't escape.

"Let them go, Blake," Aunt Martha pleaded.

Blake hit the gas and blew past the stop sign.

"You won't get away." Aunt Martha dived across his lap, jabbed at the locks. "I won't let you."

The car swerved across the middle line then veered back sharply, catapulting Cass into Jen.

"Get off me!" Blake flung his mother across the seat, sending her head bouncing off the passenger window.

"Aunt Martha!" Jen reached forward to help her.

Aunt Martha slumped back, looking dazed.

The thud of chopper blades pulled Jen's attention to the window. She squinted at the logo emblazoned on the helicopter's side—the news station's. For the first time in her life, her heart danced at the sight. If the media could find them, the police wouldn't be far behind.

In the distance, the swirl of emergency lights filled the road.

Blake slammed his brake, yanked the steering wheel a hard left and, muttering about Bellamy's ineptitude, sped away from the waiting rescue vehicles.

Jen peered out the back window. Did they see them turn? Would they follow?

Blake cursed and whipped left on a side street they'd passed moments earlier.

A fire engine blocked both lanes.

"It's Jake!" Cass pointed to a firefighter standing atop the engine, holding a hose aimed at the road.

Jen's breath caught in her chest. Sam must have heard her directions over the button cam.

Blake pulled another U-turn, coming face-to-face with a massive helicopter hovering three feet above the highway, like in the movies. Was that Sam in the cockpit? Blake skirted his SUV around it, scraping its hood on the bird's landing skids.

He gunned the gas, but two sheriff's cars and an ambulance swerved around the corner and blocked the road. Blake ramped the ditch, flipped into four-wheel drive and rammed across the rocky field.

"You can't do this!" Aunt Martha grabbed the wheel.

Together, Jen and Cass lunged for Blake's arms, restraining him from stopping her.

Martha kicked at his leg, and he suddenly stomped the brake.

Jen scarcely stopped herself from pitching over the front seat.

The driver's door burst open and Sam's gaze slammed into hers. A million messages—relief, apologies, gratitude and so much more—zinged between them in the split second before he hauled Blake from the front seat, slammed him chest-first against the hood of the car and cuffed him.

Jake jogged over in full turnout gear. "You could have let him try to run, you know. I would've loved to turn the hose on him." He opened the back door. "You ladies okay?" At their nods, he offered Cass his hand. "Let's get you out then. This vehicle's taken so many bumps we don't want anything exploding on us."

Sam handed Blake over to another officer and swept Jen into his arms. "It's over. I got you." His heart thundered against her own. "I was so afraid I'd lost you."

Closing her eyes, she savored his words. Savored the protective circle of his arms.

"Let me check her over," ordered a female voice.

Jen blinked at the petite brunette. "You look familiar."

Sam chuckled. "Meet my spitfire cousin, Sherri. The one who saved the baby."

Jake ushered Cass and Aunt Martha to the waiting ambulance. "Practically the whole family's here. We've got a couple more cousins on the fire truck."

Sam's dad joined them and slapped Sam's shoulder. "We have a couple in the police department, too. A family who's there for you, no matter what."

"Thank you," Sam said, his voice hushed.

A tall man in firefighter's gear shook Sam's hand. "Glad we could help save your girl."

Jen's heart fluttered at the reference. Did everyone think their dating act was real?

Sam's Adam's apple bobbed as the man clutched his shoulder and added, "Don't be a stranger." The man turned and swallowed her hand in his massive one. "And you must be the special lady his mother can't stop talking about?"

Sam's father beamed from ear to ear.

Oh, boy, they had a lot of explaining to do. The thought sucked the joy out of Sam's rescue. She didn't want to explain. She liked being Sam's girl. Being a part of a family that would call in the cavalry to rescue her.

"Okay, okay, Uncle Art." Sherri shooed him away. "Let me finish checking her before the whole family bowls her over." Sherri sat Jen on the ambulance's bumper and wrapped a blood pressure cuff around her arm.

Sam's gaze clung to hers, his throat still working overtime. "That was Jimmy's dad."

Knowing how healing his uncle's words must be to him, how healing the support of his entire extended family must be, Jen's eyes teared up.

Sherri ripped off the blood pressure cuff. "You're sending her pulse through the roof, Cuz. Do you mind?"

A mischievous grin curled Sam's lips. "Good to know."

A stern-looking, silver-haired guy in a gray suit approached. "Sam, we're transporting Blake Michaels. Johnson will bring you and the women in to give their statements. The mother will have to face obstruction charges." The man glanced Jen's way. "I guess your resignation still stands?"

Sam unclipped his FBI badge and slapped it into the man's palm. "Yeah."

"You resigned?" Jen gulped panic. "Because of the sniper? We cost you your job?"

"No, I chose to resign. My priorities have been screwed up for too long."

"Uh." Sherri hitched her thumb over her shoulder. "I'll just be over here counting bandages...or something."

Sam hunkered down beside Jen. "Can you ever

forgive me?" He cradled her hands. "I never meant to hurt you."

Distracted by his tender touch, the catch in his voice, she struggled to remember what she needed to forgive him for.

"I nearly died when word came that Blake had you. Nothing else mattered."

Jen pressed her hand to her thundering heart. "What are you saying?"

"Remember on the ship, when you shared your dream for your future?"

Her throat dried. "Yes."

"I saw myself in your dream. I saw our children. It was so real I could taste it."

Her heart soared. Could God really be giving her Sam to love after all?

"And it terrified me."

Her heart plummeted. "Oh."

"You were still a suspect and I had a job to do and I let you get inside my head, my heart. But fighting my feelings was like fighting a tidal wave and I soon lost the will to fight it."

The sincerity in his voice, in his eyes, spread warmth through every trembling inch of her body. "But I don't want you to give up your job for me. I—" She glanced at Cass talking with Jake and his dad and a few others who looked like they might be related. She already felt like part of Sam's family. And as wonderful as it would be to live nearby...God had shown her a better way. "I can go wherever you need to be, Sam."

He dipped his head and pressed his lips to her hands. "I need to be here."

The sweet touch of his lips, the sweeter sound of his words, flowed over her like a refreshing summer's breeze.

"This past week with you, with my family, made me question much of what my job requires. I hated hiding things from you. You accepted me at face value, even when past experience had taught you that you shouldn't. You can't imagine how much I cherished that trust, and I hated myself for not being worthy of it."

"You are the most honorable man I know."

"I haven't been all that honorable." He drew her hands to his chest. "But I do love you. With all of my heart."

"Oh, Sam—" The words clogged in her throat.

"The sheriff said there's a job here for me, if I'm interested. And I can't think of another place I'd rather be. What do you think?" He motioned to the surrounding countryside and then to his family, who were all watching them now. "Could you see yourself living here?"

"The family's kind of a package deal," Sherri warned from the side of the ambulance.

"Don't you have a baby to deliver?" Sam growled.

"Sounds like you could use my help more. You're supposed to be on one knee."

Jennifer laughed at their arguing—the kind of good-natured ribbing she experienced growing up and yearned for again.

Sherri waggled a bandage at Sam. "And where's that gorgeous ring your mom's been raving about?"

Jen gasped. "You bought me a ring?"

He dug into his front pocket, dropped to one knee and presented the very ring she'd admired in the jewelry store in Ketchikan.

"Oh, Sam." Her throat turned thick and prickly at the memory of what she'd put him through since that day.

He ducked his head, looking a little worried. "Jen, I don't want this ring to remind you of the secrets I kept, but the day I told you the truth."

Remembering his admonishment that day to cling to God, she traced his jaw with her fingertips. "More truth than you realize." Her heart swelled in wonder that God had given her Sam, too. "I love you."

He folded her in his arms and kissed her gently, sweetly. He tasted like sunshine and joy and forever. He rested his forehead against hers, and the love pouring from his gaze left her breathless.

Behind them, someone cleared his throat. "Was that a yes?"

"He didn't actually ask her," Sherri said in a stage whisper.

Sam's lips curled into a heart-stopping smile. "Will you marry me?"

Jen flung her arms around his neck and tumbled into his arms.

"Looks like a 'yes' to me," Jake bellowed, and

the next second, Cass and Sam's brother and dad and cousins and uncle swarmed them in a giant hug. "Welcome to the family."

EPILOGUE

Two months later, Sam joined Jen and Cass for a farewell tour of their family's gallery. After learning her parents' true fate, Cass had decided she wanted out, too. And despite the spate of bad publicity, David Willis stuck by his offer to buy the place. More surprising, he opted to keep the name, probably thinking its newfound notoriety might bring in more customers.

"I am going to miss working here." Cass whisked her fingers along the counter, blinking back tears. "But it wouldn't have been the same without Uncle Reggie. I still can't believe Blake hired Bellamy to kill Mom and Dad, and you, Jen."

Sam clasped Jen's hand and brought it to his lips, his heart clenching at the reminder of how close he'd come to losing her. "Thanks to Bellamy's confession, at least Blake will finally get the punishment he deserves."

"I'm glad the DA agreed to light sentences for Aunt Martha and Reggie," Jen whispered. "The thought of turning in his own son had to have torn him apart as much as losing Mom and Dad had."

"Perhaps, but Blake clearly didn't feel the same about his father," Sam said. "After slipping him a couple of roofies in Ketchikan, he stole Reggie's phone and arranged that meeting with the two of you in order to frame him."

Heaving a sigh, Cass strolled along the gallery walls and stopped in front of one of their mother's prints. "What about that sweet man who bought mom's painting at the auction? Was he really in on Blake's operation, too?"

"Blake claims that smuggling the stolen painting was the old man's idea and that he merely provided the means by convincing your uncle to contribute a couple of pieces to the ship's auction. Your uncle's purchase of the pen-and-ink drawing from the same gallery had apparently been a fluke. If we, I mean the FBI," Sam corrected himself, lovingly tracing his thumb over Jen's engagement ring, "can unravel his mob connections and convince Blake to testify against the guy, they may be able to close a few more art theft cases."

Jen curled her arm around Sam's waist and snuggled close, her warmth suffusing every corner of his heart.

He breathed a contented sigh, relishing the thought of holding her this way, every day, for the rest of their lives.

She tilted back her head, her soft gaze searching

his. "Are you sure you're ready to give up the FBI? Traveling the world? Taking down big-time—?"

He silenced her silly questions with a kiss—a deep, thorough, promise-sealing kiss. "The only travel plans I'm interested in making are for our honeymoon."

He swept his fingers through her hair and cradled the back of her head, letting the love that filled him beam from his eyes. He grinned at the blush that bloomed on her cheeks. He probably shouldn't be surprised that after dating men who were only interested in what she could give them, she'd worry he'd regret giving up his FBI career for her.

"Do you know how beautiful you are?" He let his hands drift to her neck, caressing the pulse point at her throat. "You showed me the way home. Being with you here, close to our families, maybe starting one of our own, soon—" he waggled his brows "—I can't imagine any place I'd rather be."

* * * * *

Dear Reader,

Writing this story was a fun way to revisit the Alaskan cruise my husband and I took to celebrate our twenty-fifth wedding anniversary. Of course, we didn't run into any bad guys, although my questions to the captain and crew members did raise a few eyebrows that suggested they might have been a tad concerned about me. If you've never been on a cruise, I hope the story has given you a pleasant taste of how delightful they can be. This trip was our first, but I hope not our last. Like both families in the story, we love to celebrate important milestones in special ways.

How about you? I'd love to hear about your special celebrations. You can reach me via email at: SandraOrchard@ymail.com
or at Facebook.com/SandraOrchard.

To learn about upcoming books and to read interesting bonus features—including location pics—please visit me online at www.SandraOrchard.com and sign up for my newsletter for exclusive subscriber giveaways.

Sincerely,
Sandra Orchard

Questions for Discussion

1. Jennifer yearns for a man who will love her for herself, not her money or connections, but she has a poor track record of discerning her suitors' true motives. If you were in her shoes, how might you assess whether a person's overtures of friendship were genuine?

2. On the flipside, Jennifer fears being misjudged herself. After her parents' deaths, rumors had made her life uncomfortable, and the press is always anxious for a juicy story about a wealthy heiress. But her fears compel her to remain mute about the theft she's uncovered rather than risk damage to her family's name. Have you ever been in a situation where the choice "to do the right thing" might hurt? How did you handle it? In retrospect, would you respond differently today?

3. Sam is tormented by his part in his young cousin's death and out of a twisted sense of loyalty moves far away from his family rather than be a constant reminder of their loss. Do you struggle to forgive yourself, or others, for your, or their, role in a tragedy? What steps might you take to help restore the relationship and find healing?

4. Both the Steele and the Robbins families booked their Alaskan cruises to celebrate milestones in

their lives. Do you do something special to celebrate such milestones? Why or why not?

5. Jennifer's faith is strong, yet she grows to realize that she's been looking to other people—a husband, a family—to give her a sense of completeness and to make her happy. Have you struggled with looking to others, rather than God, to satisfy and fulfill you?

6. Sam's job sometimes requires him to be deceptive in order to catch criminals. Do you think deception in such cases is justified? Why or why not?

7. In trying to uncover who attacked Jennifer, Sam makes use of various tracking methods such as the cruise cards, surveillance cameras and credit card purchases ashore. Individual privacy is becoming increasingly encroached upon by such means. How do you feel about that? Do they make you feel safer?

8. After Jennifer spends time playing games with Sam's family, happy memories of such times with her own family replace more recent, bitter memories of how the art gallery overshadowed their family life. What kind of memories are you creating with your loved ones?

9. Despite the evidence against her sister, Jennifer wants to believe the best about Cass. Do you tend

to believe the best or the worst of others? Has your tendency left you burned or for the better?

10. Having one's drink drugged is one of many dangers women may face when out in public. What steps do you take to protect yourself from opportunists?

LARGER-PRINT BOOKS!

GET 2 FREE LARGER-PRINT NOVELS PLUS 2 FREE MYSTERY GIFTS

Love Inspired

Larger-print novels are now available...

ReaderService.com

Manage your account online!

- Review your order history
- Manage your payments
- Update your address

*We've designed
the Harlequin® Reader Service
website just for you.*

Enjoy all the features!

- Reader excerpts from any series
- Respond to mailings and special monthly offers
- Discover new series available to you
- Browse the Bonus Bucks catalog
- Share your feedback

Visit us at:
ReaderService.com